"Seas and stars, oce vessel as we *do stupid s* and punched a button whose only label was WARNING. Space distorted in front of the *Wadja* as she accelerated and twisted to dodge shots from the pursuing patrol craft. Some that just barely missed the pirate vessel were swallowed, torn apart, unmade as they entered the distortion ahead. Hock stared at it, willing it to open into a full rift before the *Wadja* was on top of it.

The fighters caught up and loosed a volley at the pirate vessel, which Tenta just barely managed to avoid. They screamed past, spreading out to try to circle for another run.

Almost everyone stared forward at one of the fighters and, beyond it, the increasingly distorting point in space, as the *Wadja* looked to be on the losing side of a game of chicken against the natural laws of the universe. Liz alone was looking back at the captain. "If we die, I haunt you."

The rift finally tore open, the force of it shredding part of the fighter and sucking the rest through. Hock cackled. "Hey-HEY! Fair enough, Liz. *Allons-y!*"

Liz stared at Hock in bewilderment. The prismatic maelstrom reflected across his cackling face as the *Wadja* tore into the unknown.

Also by Andrew Bugenis

Firestorm

HOW WE **STOPPED** THE **DESTROYERS**

ANDREW BUGENIS

Jean,

Thanks so much for your support!
(I considered drawing something almost-obscene but decided against it. If you want I can do so when we finally hang out.)

—Bater

A. B.

This is a work of fiction. All of the characters, organizations, and events portrayed in this story are either products of the author's imagination or used fictitiously.

HOW WE STOPPED THE DESTROYERS

Copyright © 2022 Andrew Bugenis

All rights reserved, including the right to reproduce this book, or portions thereof, in any form.

Cover art by Paul Youll
Cover design by Jeff Brown
Ebook layout by Martin Lejeune

A Press Enter Publishing paperback

Bugenis, Andrew
    How We Stopped the Destroyers / Andrew Bugenis
    ISBN 9798846323230

First Edition: October 2022

INDEX

HOW WE STOPPED THE DESTROYERS

Act One
p. 1

Act Two
p. 69

Act Three
p. 129

THE TREASON DUOLOGY

Prelude to How We Stopped the Destroyers

Preface
p. 207

What's Treason Between Friends?
p. 209

Mutual Treason
p. 220

*When a fledgling culture reaches for the stars,
they must be careful;
what awaits them may be protection,
or destruction;
order,
or chaos;
a community ready to welcome them
or a force of darkness.*

*The endless cycles of history tell us
that it is the responsibility of all
who wish to survive
to push back against the dark,
and to stop those who would destroy.*

ACT ONE

Chapter One

Eliyas considered himself a "social physicist".

This didn't mean that he got along with people. In general, he couldn't stand them. And it had nothing to do with sociology—a softer science you couldn't find even if it were performed by a half dozen of the gelatinous boubana, he felt, and not at all worth his valuable time. Instead, when he said that, he meant that he considered what people might *do* with the discoveries and advancements he made in his labs. Indeed, it seemed like his disdain for people made him more predisposed to consider how other supposedly sapient beings might misuse something, or overlook something basic.

Considerations which, more often than not, fed into a loop that lowered his estimation of people a little more each time.

The jendeer were a prime example that continuously caused Eliyas such frustration. On the surface, they were a vaguely feline species that had monopolized interstellar travel for millennia, keeping the technology secret and operating large Jump Ferries on which the entire galactic community traveled. Roughly every six hours, every Jump Ferry would open a subspace rift to its next destination, and through this "interval" system they dictated the steady drumbeat of commerce and simplified travel. Genius, Eliyas conceded; one could certainly appreciate such an economic stranglehold, even if one resented how total their monopoly had been.

Then one considered that the interval likely arose because subspace jumps gave off low levels of "mu-radiation", which, if allowed to reach a high concentration, would attract the Destroyers, a force of mythical proportions that had faded into history through nothing more than dumb luck. A force that would have stayed in history had humanity not stolen subspace drive technology and started jumping off-interval with drives that emitted far more mu-radiation than jendeer drives did.

The return of the Destroyers, and the subsequent pitched attempt to drive them off, resulted in victory at the cost of untold destroyed ships in Earth's orbit, and the jendeer proposal that humanity stop pursuing subspace tech and to leave it to the jendeer to continue to orchestrate the interval—all so their engineers wouldn't have to put the extra work into their technology. They'd gotten mu-rad emissions down to "good enough" rather than "gone", and that just wasn't good enough. So Eliyas had little time for jendeer engineers.

Why, then, was he the one stuck grilling this jendeer historian?

Because nobody else thought it important.

"I have other people speaking with physicists," said Eliyas in exasperated response to said historian asking him essentially the same question. "I just want... the historical perspective. What is your *culture's* experience with mu-radiation, with the Destroyers. It's a big-picture perspective that helps us grasp the context of the work you've done and might identify blind spots for us to start our own work in."

"That's fine, Dr. Omarov, but before we begin I need to reiterate that records from the time of the first Destroyer incursion are sketchy at best," said Zandkhy, and Eliyas' estimation of jendeer historians continued to sink to somewhere near his estimation of sociologists.

Eliyas dropped his notebook to the sofa cushion beside him. "How does a modern society just lose its history? How does it forget the biggest existential threat it had ever faced?"

"You must understand, that was more than two thousand years ago." Zan was seated on an armchair, kitty-corner to him around a small glass coffee table in Eliyas' office. "Possibly three thousand, we don't even know. The Fall of the Enlightenment itself wiped any electronic records on most of our cultural centers."

"Right, when you lost everything and decided to just start counting the years from zero again."

"That's not—" Zandkhy stopped himself, closed his eyes, and put a paw up to his face. He took a deep breath, then continued more slowly, "We first reset our epoch because society had undergone such a great change. We can pin down that first date in the old calendar, during the 547th Year of the Peaceful Reign of the Enlighten—" He cut himself off when he saw Eliyas roll his eyes. "Well, yes, to be sure it was time to change how we marked dates anyway. Five hundred years away from Jendaaren and those of us in space still marked time by who had been in power when the first colonies were established, even as those on the homeworld kept marking new dynasties. So, yes, we reset our calendar." His tone hardened again. "Then after some period of time, we restarted again. That period, referred to as the Enlightened Kingdom, is generally accepted to be about three hundred years but we don't have the records to confirm that. Such a thing happens when half of your homeworld is glassed and the Kingdom gets relegated to the history books."

Eliyas softened; he didn't like people and scorned most professions, sure, but he wasn't an *asshole* about it. "I'm sorry," he said. "I was out of line. Please understand how difficult it is for us to comprehend. We lost a lot of our own history around the same time, but that was... ancient history, literally. Great civilizations collapsed and empires turned into scattered villages led by warchiefs. We thought a spacefaring civilization would be beyond that."

"No," Zan intoned wistfully. "I studied that period of human history for a semester, the parallels between your European Dark Ages and our own Post-Enlightenment era are quite fascinating. I'll spare you the more granular details," he added quickly, as Eliyas' resting grouch face slid back into position, "but to oversimplify: your Roman Empire was so great that when it began to fail, it did so slowly, its institutions fading so slowly that people may not have realized they were living during the decline of a great empire. Even after it fell, there were still roads connecting places, you could still travel by sea. The Enlightened Kingdom was much the same, establishing trade routes and culture, economy and science, ensuring the continuance of space travel and Jump Ferries even after the fall of the political and military hierarchy." He cleared his throat uncomfortably. "Of course, the calamity that ended the Kingdom was more sudden than the fall of the Roman Empire, but the idea of individual institutions outlasting the greater whole is the same."

Zan lapped some water from a wide glass before starting again. "Details of the calamity that befell us were spread by word of mouth, and susceptible to the sorts of distortions that such a transmission vector entail, as more concrete records were destroyed. Do you know," he added, frustratingly unable to resist a tangent, "that the reason my species prefers to use discrete data chips rather than onboard storage is that chips keep our information more decentralized, as opposed to network servers that would be easy to destroy again?" As if to illustrate, he plucked a data chip from his neckpiece and plugged it into his tablet, bringing up his notes.

"That doesn't help when you still have a lot of them in one physical location. Does the phrase 'Library of Alexandria' mean anything to you?"

Zan's eyes widened, and then he tilted his head, conceding the point. "Anyhow. Communication broke down and we stayed on the interval out of habit and superstition. Sometimes a colony would disappear off the charts—it's assumed that those lost colonies tried jumping off-interval, and were met by the Destroyers' wrath." He took a deep breath. "Habit and superstition, quite literally, kept us alive. Do not discount it."

"I don't discount it," Eliyas said. "But they have their place. I seem to remember something about remedies in the Dark Ages needing to be accompanied by certain prayers. The prayers didn't do the healing, of course, but saying three Hail Marys or whatever while you mixed up some medicine was more accessible than counting out... however many seconds it takes to say three Hail Marys. Look, my point is— habit and superstition served you well, but it is past time to move past them both." He reached for the notebook he'd long abandoned on the sofa next to him. "So while my colleagues work with your own physicists to understand the theory behind subspace travel, it has for some reason fallen to me to ask some basic questions about your sketchy history."

"Yes, of course," said Zan. He leaned back in the

armchair, wiggling a bit to keep from sitting on his tail. "Well. With no guarantees that I can answer, what would you like to know?"

"Well, what happened? 'Everything changed when the Destroyers attacked' isn't good enough. To the best of your species' recollection, passed down through word of mouth, surviving electronic databases, or through paper records—hell, pottery records, if it helps—how did the first war with the Destroyers go?"

"Well. We invented subspace jump technology in the 231st year of the Peaceful Reign of Enlightened, and in the time after that we had met two other species, the shiwiik and the qronth, each confined to their home star systems. So the Destroyers showed up after we'd been the only ones jumping around the galaxy for at least half a century, and for... a fleeting moment, I have to assume that we were thrilled to see another interstellar society. Uh..." He swiped through his own notes, trying to stay ahead of Eliyas' impatience. "Dah duh-dah duh-dahhh... okay, so reconstructed from some oral tellings of the event and recontextualized from 'looking upon the face of a god' type stuff, it seems that when the Destroyers first jumped into our home star system, they hung there in space, mysterious and enigmatic. They 'spoke the languages of the gods that we learned'—near as we can tell, this means they were bleeding mu-radiation from the jump, maybe even more than we do while jumping. We had discovered mu-rad during the small war that had caused us to finally drop the Peaceful Reign calendar, and had detection buoys as early-warning systems."

"Those early drive systems must have absolutely hemorrhaged mu-radiation whenever they opened a subspace rift."

"We don't have any numbers, but it's likely, yes. Nowadays, those mu-rad buoys still exist, and it's how we found that humans were jumping off-interval. Anyhow, we tried to speak to the new arrivals, but all attempts at communication failed. I assume we tried various mathematical constants and so forth in addition to good old, 'Hello, how do you do, we hope you come in peace.' And after—*oof*, 'days numbering thirty', similar to your species' early use of the number forty to say 'a long time'—after some time, the Destroyers awoke, and started slaughtering us."

"So. Attempts at communication were made."

"I—yes."

"All you had to say," Eliyas grumbled. "So began the glassing of Jendaaran."

"Yes, indeed. And during the next—*ahem*—'thirty' years, it would continue. 'The gods listened for where their language was spoken, and would smite those who dared so boldly.' They probably had their own mu-rad detection system and were tracing it to find targets. And then, a couple of Jump Ferries came up with the interval. No hard research behind it, not that we can find at any rate, just... let's space out our jumps, and do it at the same time, so neither mu-rad signature is stronger. 'The steady drum-beat babble of the divine lexicon.' Gotta love when poets get their tongues on history."

"I hate it. No offense."

"None taken. Drives me absolutely up the wall. But it's what we have."

"I get it, though. Get one angry person in a field playing Marco Polo, except they don't get to solicit replies; just every six hours, everyone around them shouts, 'Polo!' and then goes silent again. Maddening but what can you do about it?"

"I'll have to take your word on it. The name is familiar to me, but not from a part of human history I've studied."

If Eliyas were a people person, he'd offer to teach

Zandkhy the game. But, he wasn't, and he wouldn't. So he simply said, "Anything else?"

"Sometime during the Fall, we discovered mu-radiation polarization. Ah..." Zan again swiped through his notes; not being a physicist, he didn't know the technical terms off the top of his head. "It turns out that when the Destroyers dropped into a system, their mu-rad would be, ah, 'transversely polarized'. We could never manage to generate transverse mu-rad, only normal, or 'longitudinal' if you need an unbiased retronym for it. Again, it's our buoys' ability to detect transverse mu-rad that let us know you were under attack."

"And we are, as ever, grateful to your fleet for their assistance once you knew what was going on. So. The Destroyers showed up, hung out for a bit while you tried to establish communications, and upon your failure they proceeded to knock you back to a spacefaring dark age. Along the way you discovered transverse mu-radiation, decided that centralizing data was a bad idea, and began using the subspace jump interval that is still in use today, all while cursing the existence of poets."

"That about sums it up. I mean, if not for the poets we might have had even less to go on, but... never become a historian, Dr. Omarov, you haven't the temperament for it."

"Tell me something I don't know."

"Well, you don't seem to know that most of the economic players of my culture would rather you didn't pursue this at all."

"I know," Eliyas grumbled, "I just don't particularly *care*. Neither does anyone else. Your culture against a couple dozen others, and without your help we'd do it anyway, just with more collateral damage, like last time.

"It's about the principle of the thing. Imagine what could be done if jumps weren't hampered by the threat of the

Destroyers! The money to be made, the speed of societal mingling, the... whatever people care about." Eliyas waved his hand, dismissing the details. "To be quite honest with you, I just welcome the challenge. There is a problem to be solved that your species hasn't bothered fully solving, basically since time immemorial. So I want to solve it. Get rid of mu-rad entirely, not just down to a 'safe level' but *gone*. Then the politicians and business magnates can figure out how society will look in that post-interval world. I'm sorry, but one way or the other, your species' iron grip on galactic commerce is coming to an end."

"And that might be for the best," the historian replied. "It will be calamitous for the status quo, but to take a long view... things have been the same for far too long. It might be good for the galactic situation to get shaken up... presuming this doesn't lead to unfettered warfare."

"Well, what major scientific advancement hasn't been weaponized sooner or later."

The jendeer considered Eliyas. "What a human thing to say."

And that's enough. "Well, thank you for your time, Zandkhy. I hope you uncover more in your continuing research into the era."

Eliyas saw Zan out the door then returned to his desk. He looked at the scant few lines he'd scribbled in his notebook.

"This could have been an email..."

Chapter 2

"Hey-hey!" the captain cried as he quite literally flew through the tight, tangled passageways of the ship. The meter-long kikan twisted and turned like an aquatic animal, but most of his thrust came from the air rushing out of his float bladder. To bipeds stuck on the ground, the kikan species sometimes looked chaotic and erratic, but they could be quite graceful when they wanted.

"Hel'kef, secure that rigging! Snetzk, close up the gun housing! We head out in five!"

Captain Hock Corven *reveled* in being chaotic and erratic. He'd grown up on a pirate vessel, but it was always so *dour*. Then he saw some old human pirate vids—now *they* knew how to live the profiteering life! He vowed to live up to that ideal, and when he got his own ship, that's just what he did. Oh, yes, he owed the humans a lot—he was an entrepreneur, and he woke up every day excited to get to work.

A shame he had almost no humans on his crew. They usually found the air too thick for their liking and the gravity too low. Well, their loss!

He coasted for a moment, his float bladder empty, sinking towards the deck and approaching a corner in the passageway. He grinned, swung to the outside of the corner, then BOOMPH! He inflated to nearly spherical in a fraction of a second, careening off the bulkheads and accelerating around the corner, nearly bowling over a long-necked junior crewman who was carrying a box of equipment.

"Cap'n!" yelped the crewman, getting out of the way, as Hock cackled his way past. The kikan diverted his puff bladder to his float bladder, refilling it and using the extra to accelerate down the passageway again. A few more "Hey-hey"s and calls to the crew and he arrived on the bridge, back down to his usual size.

"How's our registry?" he called out, and swam his way to his station at the center of the cluttered mayhem of the bridge of the *Wadja*. His coat fluttered behind him, far baggier than was strictly necessary for any kikan who adopted the affectation.

"Updated with local authority, has been propagating for the last two intervals. You're currently on the bridge of the independently registered salvage vessel *Grey Bird*."

"Fantastic! Boring! I love it. Drive signature?"

"Fry outdid himself this time. The crazy jendeer fixed our usual modulation but then rigged it so engine number two just cuts out every fifteen seconds or so!"

Hock blinked his big eyes. "Why not?! We can disable that if we gotta bolt, right?"

"Sure thing! Unless the modulation fix stresses something else and cuts out the other two engines."

"Tell him I don't want that fix to be permanent, it helps me sleep at night. Okay, Liz, how's the crew?"

His first mate looked at her board and the last pink light illuminated. She turned back to him and said, "Crew is ready to go when you say, Cap'n," then grabbed a tricorn hat off her console and tugged it onto her head.

Liz was the only human on the crew, and while everyone else tolerated or played along with Hock's vision of piratical chaos, she seemed to take to it as fervently as he did. She wore a similarly flamboyant coat, puffy pants, tall boots, a loose shirt with a brown leather bodice that still allowed her a full range of motion, and when the fancy hit her, the tricorn. (She'd originally gotten it for Hock as a gift, but the first time he'd puffed while wearing it the thing went flying and got lodged in a run of power conduits. Headgear and kikan didn't typically mix well.)

"I say, I say!" Hock said, looking forward to the score in front of him. "Let's get moving. We've got some salvage to grab!"

* * *

Pirates typically operated within a single star system, taking advantage of the vast scales involved in space travel to fall upon a ship, take what they fancied, and get out before local authorities could catch on. They almost never took their operations interstellar; suggest to a pirate captain that they take their ship—wanted, with a bounty on nearly every head on board—on a Jump Ferry—the only way to travel between the stars and typically teeming with authorities both civil and mercantile—and you'd be laughed right off the vessel. Alive, if you were lucky.

Any spacefarer worth their salt understood that the Jendeeri Stellar Economic Union kept a stranglehold on all travel, and while treaties had long dictated that anyone with the cash could hop a ride on a Jump Ferry—including even military fleets in a recognized war—nobody else had the subspace tech to make a jump.

Well. Nobody but the humans. As with many things, they had recently proven to be a notable exception.

Nevertheless, the jendeer monopoly on travel made it dangerous to be a pirate. Pirate vessels, by their very nature, existed to disrupt the mechanisms of economy, and the Jendeeri Stellar *Economic* Union dictated that such craft were about the only ones they wouldn't transport, effectively leaving them stuck in whatever system they were currently sailing. If security got too tight, there was nowhere to go but to some empty rock within the system and hope the heat dissipated before the crew died of hunger or, worse, mutinied. The Trappist system was getting too crowded, and while Hock would never publicly admit to fear, and only rarely admit to caution, he did see the value of prudence. He had relocated twice before in his career; once when he got his own ship and needed to sail a different system than his old mentor, and once a few years ago when the Bou system got too hot. Relocation was hard, and there was a lot of luck involved, but it was doable.

The current operation wasn't quite a relocation, but the logistics were the same. The *Wadja* approached the Jump Ferry, paid for a berth, and her pilot guided her to the assigned rigging inside the otherwise hollow ship. A tense hour passed while they waited for the interval; so many ships were crowded around them, and it seemed like any one of them would recognize the (to its captain) massively famous pirate vessel, scourge of the system.

Hock's ego was almost bruised, a bit, a tiny bit, when they went unrecognized, and jumped without incident, and ships started filing out of the Jump Ship. Half an hour later, and they were again in empty space. They'd made it.

* * *

There were so many artificial satellites in orbit of this planet that its deep gravitational well had accrued a large number of artificial ex-satellites, and the local authorities had recently put out a call for contractors to help remove the dangerous space junk from their skies. The humble Captain Hollis of the independent salvager *Grey Bird* had been more than happy to answer their call, and was now off to work, the captain having vocally hoped to scrape enough out of the sky to cover his expenses.

In truth, once the *Wadja* was away from the transfer station and anyone who might care to pay them even a speck of attention, she changed course for a different dark patch of sky, and lay in wait.

Liz lounged at her post, her feet up, bobbing one up and down, as if trying to twirl the hat resting on her toes. Hock had noticed only a few species with such a pronounced difference between simply at rest and lounging, and humans lounged better than most. Liz Bewick was an artist of the form.

She lolled her head to the side, looking vaguely in the direction of the jendeer at the gunnery station. "Threm, I'm askin' again."

"I told ya not t' ask again!"

"I'm askin' again."

"My guy said this shipment's got the big stuff. Hush-hush. Real quiet like. They wanna get stuff t' their fancy new lab, they gotta ship it. They ain't messin' with off-interval jumps no more, so it's gotta be at L1 for the next 'un."

"Not L4 or L5."

"What, out in the middle of nowhere where some pirate can jump 'em?" Everyone laughed. "Nah, they got their own Jump Ferry but it's hoppin' from L1 just like everyone else."

"You trust when your guy says it's got the big stuff?"

"Trust 'im more than half the reprobates on the ship—no offense, Cap'n."

"None taken, Threm! None taken at all." Hock wished he could lounge; the next part would work so much better if he could, for a moment, sit up from a good lounge and stare Threm in the eyes. As it was, he floated a touch higher above his station and leaned forward a bit. "Just know it's those untrustworthy scalliwags what gonna be hangin' your tender orange pelt out the airlock if your guy doesn't come through for ya."

"Aw, hell," said Ssswoorssepp at sensors. The plishken's quills rippled down her small, hexapedal body. "Cap'n, I know you're enjoyin' the suspense an' all, but waitin's done. I'm 'fraid we got a ping." She looked at Threm. "Single vessel. Barge. Or, I mean, bigass warship. But hopefully barge."

"Still suspenseful!" cried Captain Corven. He puffed up a bit, then let it back out. "Snap to! Stay powered down 'til they're nice and close."

Everyone sat up (or the equivalent; the kikan crew members floated more attentively), refocusing on their stations. Liz kicked her hat up and caught it, placing it on her head and she sat at the ready by her internal comms station. "All hands, long range contact. Stand by for orders."

"Can't wait 'til we don't hafta stay in low-power when stalkin' a score," said Ssswoo. "Gonna be a game-changer."

"If Threm's guy came through, yeah." Liz winked at the scowling jendeer.

Silence reigned as the contact approached. "Two fighters," breathed Sssworrssepp, "Solvable," said Threm, and that was it until it was almost in range.

"What do you think, Liz?" asked Hock in a mock whisper. "Full drama?"

"No, nono, tone it down. This is a human crew, you go

full drama with them, they're more likely to think you're trying too hard and won't take you seriously."

"Not necessarily a bad thing. So no uplighting?"

"*God* no. Keep it to the spines. Oh, and by *no* means should I ever be visible."

"What, are you wanted here?"

"I mean, who isn't, but no. Dressed like this? They'll be laughing too hard to be any help at all."

"Spines it is. Fovak, spin me up a channel." The kikan comms tech got to work. "And for the record, first mate, most of us aren't wanted in Earth space." He clapped his fins together and rubbed them, an incredibly human gesture. "Who wants to change that?"

Chapter Three

"Did I miss something?" asked Eliyas, looking around the lab. People were bustling about, packing all manner of things into boxes.

"Never have I known someone to say so much about so little," bemoaned Siobhan—Dr. Doyle to most—as she passed, packing some of her computer equipment away.

"I know the feeling," Eliyas grumbled. He opened his mouth to repeat his question when Siobhan continued, oblivious.

"Are all jendeer like that, or do they just not like us poking at what they *laughably* consider 'proven science'?"

"Siobhan, what—okay, there's a story there. Hold it for a sec. What's going on?"

"Oh—you didn't get the memo?"

"What memo, Doctor."

"Don't you 'Doctor' me." She set a tablet into a foam divider, then swiped through messages on her watch. "You weren't in your meeting that long, this came in this morning."

"It felt like a week." Eliyas made a show of rolling up his

sleeves and checking his bare wrists, then patting his pockets. "Want to just skip the condescension and fill me in?"

"What's good for the goose is good for the gander, *Doctor.*"

"Dr. Patel!" called Eliyas over Siobhan's head. "What are—"

Siobhan smacked his arm. "Leave him alone. Suresh, ignore Dr. Omarov. I'll handle him." When the team had first been assembled, Eliyas had bristled at the notion of being "handled", but he'd gotten used to it. Siobhan took the tablet back out and flipped through it. "We're to pack up—we're being relocated to Alpha Point tomorrow."

"Pack up? We're in the middle of working here."

"No, Eliyas, we've just *started* working here. We're going to be doing the rest of our work on theoretical physics that could trigger an immune response from the universe out away from civilization."

Eliyas looked at Siobhan in annoyed disbelief. Fortunately, her own face showed the same mixture of emotions. "The universe's immune response, that's what he said. Along with a lot of other conjecture. Absolutely none of which was needed. Tell you what, you sit there nicely and stay out of everyone's way while I pack and fill you in on what little usable information we got on the theory of subspace. Then we'll go to your office and you get to tell me what you learned."

"I found out nothing of value and don't need someone underfoot."

"Win-win. So you commence with the sitting nicely and the listening up." She dropped the tablet back into the box as Eliyas sat on an office chair. "So. Some of this the original Alpha Point team found out while they were supervising the engineers, but they weren't the best in the field. Just the lowest security risks. All they needed to do was make sure the people scaling the tech down and making material substitutions didn't miscarry a zero or something. If we'd have been on the team in the first place, maybe the Battle of Earth wouldn't have happened."

Eliyas scoffed at the terminally science-fiction-sounding "Battle of Earth" but otherwise kept quiet.

Siobhan popped another box into form and started emptying the drawers of her desk into it. Mostly scratch pads and pen scribbles; if Eliyas' own desk drawers were any indication, the box would probably go unopened once at Alpha Point. "While the jendeer haven't actively developed the technology in a couple millennia, they have what *they* consider to be a decent understanding of how it works. They say that when a subspace drive opens a rift, it sends a signal into a lower layer of the universe—'sub'space—that is like a source code, data layer of reality."

"That's—"

"I'm not done. I'm dropping this all on you at once, then you can be incredulous." She thunked a stack of loose sheets on the desk a few times to square it up then dropped it into the box. "The signal navigates the coordinate sector of subspace, basically scrolling through an index of coordinates, and when it finds a match, it then uses that to open up a corresponding rift at the destination. It inputs a temporary command that forces the operating system of the universe to consider the two points temporarily adjacent; then after transit, it closes the rifts and dummies out the command."

Eliyas looked at Siobhan in shock. "That's... not only is that *not* how the universe works—"

Siobhan threw her arms in the air. "That's what I said!"

"—but if it *were* how it works, that is *grossly* irresponsible. Making live adjustments to the source code of the universe— what if the adjustment gets made permanent, what if you not just link but *change* some coordinates, what if—jeez, what if you just *deleted* some coordinates? If you could edit the source code of the universe, you could solve any encroaching military threat by just *deleting them*."

"Be a really handy way to deal with the Destroyers, once we figured out where they're coming from, huh."

"You don't just—you don't just mess with stuff like that to make things *convenient* for you."

"Eliyas, no matter how it works, subspace travel probably *does* egregiously break the laws of physics for the sake of convenience."

Eliyas took a moment to get his breathing under control. He was unsure whether to blame his typical anger and contempt for fools, or if he was having a panic attack at the remote possibility that that was how subspace travel actually operated.

"Okay. But that is *not* how the universe works."

"Nope."

"There is no *data layer* underneath physical space that sets basic parameters."

"Probably not."

"There—*probably* not?"

"We never thought to look. But if there were, what good would a physical coordinate system be?"

"Matter and energy exist and they can only move so fast and everything else follows naturally from there."

"I mean..."

"Simplifying here, Siobhan."

"Then sure."

"Okay." He took another deep breath. "And what about mu-radiation?"

"You're gonna love this."

"I'm almost positive I won't."

"Mu-radiation is the way that the contents of the data layer are read. It's not like there's a spreadsheet sitting there in space, the data layer is pure energy, so *of course* any glimpse of the data layer takes the form of an energy wave."

"I was right. I don't love it. I, in fact, hate it."

"And yet you get to grouse about it immediately. I had to hold my tongue."

"I dealt with a historian of a civilization whose civilization lost its history. I have no sympathy."

"Just wait 'til you hear what they think about transverse mu-rad."

Eliyas buried his head in his hands and took a deep, shuddering breath. "I am not ready."

"Longitudinal mu-rad is reading the contents of the data layer. Transverse mu-rad is the write operation."

"What—no. Stop it. They do not believe this."

"If their physicists, all of whom I vetted as actually being at the top of their field, were telling the truth, then yes."

"Why would we see evidence of the write operation only when the *Destroyers* open a subspace rift?" Eliyas' eyes boggled. "It's like they had an idea and didn't bother thinking about it for a second longer than it took to put it into a coherent sentence."

"The explanation goes more in-depth than that but it ends up just sounding like some bad fan-fiction. There'll be a writeup on the project board later."

"Fiction, that has to be it. They sold you a lie and are hiding information on anything Destroyer-related because they're scared."

"No, I didn't get that sense." Siobhan finally finished clearing out her desk and stacked the boxes, then leaned on the corner of it, looking at Eliyas. "I honestly believe that they are too complacent to challenge what they consider to be settled science. You want to talk bad historians? They haven't made any real advancements in the physical sciences in decades if not centuries. Their top scientists just learn what came before so they can puppet it back." Her gaze started to wander, and found some nondescript spot in the wall to glare into. "And they *especially* aren't going to work on it now, now that they remember why they stopped poking the subspace bear in the first place. The most original work they've done in their lives is digging through old texts and deciphering them to say, 'This is how the ancients thought subspace worked,' and just accepting it, without doing any independent verification to back it up. So speculation got passed down as the rule of law." She refocused on Eliyas. "So yeah. Tell me again about your awful historians."

Eliyas leaned back, a grimace on his face. "Do you really want me to tell you about it?"

"*God*, no. Throw it in a node on the project board and I'll read it when I've managed to regain some shred of faith in sapiency."

"Which will be about three days from never." Eliyas groaned as he stood up and went back to the door. "So subspace travel works because it does and frankly nobody has any clue why." Siobhan nodded in agreement. "Then... I guess we do their science for them and figure it out ourselves."

"Yeah. Don't get me wrong," said Siobhan, "I'm glad we know the consequences of bad subspace use. If we would've known it from the start, maybe the Destroyers wouldn't have popped back up. But now that we have that context, and some best practices for use... we're on our own when it comes to figuring out the science."

"Right. And only then, when we've done the work they should have done centuries ago in figuring out how it works, *then* we can work on the mu-rad problem and try to discover what purpose the Destroyers serve."

"If they serve a purpose at all. We know nothing about them."

"Yes, if—ugh, see, *that's* how it happens." Eliyas rubbed his forehead. "They talk so much ridiculous tripe that you start to just accept the fringe assumptions of their less outlandish claims."

"Right. When you start with, 'Immune response isn't their purpose,' you get tricked into assuming there's a purpose in the first place." Siobhan lightly shoved Eliyas out of her office. "Go pack and yell about it to yourself for a while. We'll talk about it on the trip to Alpha Point and get some proper working hypotheses going. Until then... just, don't yell at anyone, okay?"

Eliyas harrumphed and looked at Suresh, who noticed and then ducked his head, busying himself with something else. "No guarantees," said Eliyas, turning down the hall, "if I run across another jendeer eager to share their stupid ideas."

Chapter 4

"Now listen here! You can deny what is happening all you like, you can quiver in your, ah, boots, but I will not be mocked!"

Out of the corner of his eye, Hock saw Liz wince and mime turning a dial down. Well, too bad, he was in it now. He'd tried to play it cool, but the moment the video connection was established, these humans had *laughed!* It probably had something to do with his resemblance to some Earth creature. Well, he wouldn't stand for it. Captain Hock Corven could be ignored; that was fine. He could deal with being underestimated. But to be found *adorable?* Absolutely not.

"Oh, no, of *course,*" said the human barge captain with a smile. "You are the fearsome pirate captain and I am but a humble merchant whose hold is full of *secret and classified technology,* all yours to plunder. If you don't mind, little guy, we're on a bit of a schedule here, and you, well, my little scamp, why don't you just run along before we put a hot tip in to the Terran Intelligence Agency about you coming across some *highly sensitive* information?"

The human seemed to enjoy playing off the nature of his cargo as being equally as implausible as everything else he (mistakenly) thought of the situation. If Hock were an amateur, it'd give him pause—a pause that a sharp opponent would take for weakness.

Hock wasn't an amateur. He was, however, angry, and prideful. "*That's* it. Captain, at this point whether or not you are carrying what I think you're carrying is immaterial. We will board, inventory, and take what we please. I give you until the count of two to transmit your manifest and make things simple."

"Aw, not three? How will I ever comply with only a two count, little fella?"

"Gunnery teams, stand by," Hock heard Threm say quietly.

"One."

"Okay, folks, tiny here wants to play. Sortie our escort, let's get moving. Captain? It has been an absolute delight. If you'll excuse us, we have a schedule to keep."

The screen went blank, revealing the forward viewport and beyond it, Earth. "Two. Jam comms."

"Comms jammed. I don't think they took you seriously enough to report us while they had you on the line."

"Their loss. Threm?"

"Gunnery teams, fire on incoming fighters!"

"Take us to their stern, Tenta."

"Aye, Cap'n!"

The *Wadja* accelerated hard as thumping guns began to reverberate through the hull. One fighter, caught unawares, was immediately winged by the timed-fuse ballistics and spiraled away, and the second fighter broke off its attack run, allowing the *Wadja* to get behind the barge.

"Transmitting engine specs to weapons."

"Thanks, Ssswoo. Configuring EM torpedoes. Tube 1 evacuated. Ready to fire."

"Fire!" The larger vessel tried to turn, to keep her engines away from the more nimble pirate schooner, but it was no use. A meatier *thwump* passed through the ship. "Torpedo launched from tube 1. Three seconds to impact. Keep that fighter away!" Threm yelled, switching from reporting to the bridge to directing his teams.

The fighter dove in, heedless of the miniature explosions around it, and fired at the path of the torpedo. There was a bright flash.

"Ssswoo, status?"

"Premature EM detonation, sensors are... holdin'. Fighter... is ballistic. Leaving AO. Barge engines... didn't take the full hit but looks close enough. Cascade failure, looks like we shorted out enough that the rest either overloaded or got shut down."

"Fan-*tast*-ic, great job!" Hock swam a quick circle in the air. "Liz, send someone out to plant a backup charge by their engines in case they try to start 'em up again, stay here to coordinate. Tenta, bring us in to board. Boarding teams, suit up!"

* * *

Hock, held aloft by an anti-grav generator, led the way across the umbilical onto the barge. One of the team hacked open the barge's door, and the lighter human-standard air pressure sucked him forward. He quickly swam to maintain position as the pressures equalized, and found himself looking into a half dozen gun barrels.

He wasn't worried. He had twice that behind him.

"You fought well," Hock lied, "but this will go one of two ways." He drifted forward slightly, towards the captain, whose stern look belied his displeasure at having underestimated him. "First, you shoot me, and I am *dramatically* injured, and in their *endless* grief my crew kills your crew with superior firepower, and we take what we want. Second, you stand down, and we take what we want. Now, I don't know about you, but *I* would prefer—"

"I'll stand down if it means I never have to hear another melodramatic word from your fishy little mouth."

Hock's eyes widened in mock surprise, an unspoken *who, me?* that he hoped carried between species. But he bobbed in assent, and the barge captain signaled for his men to stand down. "We will collect your team's firearms," said Hock, "and you will lead us to your hold. If you have a manifest it will expedite the process. Any suspected delay will result in previous promises of physical harm being carried out. Your firearms will be returned to you when we vacate your vessel." The dull tone was unfamiliar from his own mouth but Hock took a sort of perverse pleasure in using it against the barge captain, who gritted his teeth and pulled out a tablet.

The captains and their respective crews made their way to the hold that made up ninety percent of the vessel. The heavier gravity dragged on Hock and the lighter pressure made him feel bloated, but the anti-grav held.

Inside the hold were stacks of cargo containers as far as the eye could see. Cursing Threm's informant under his breath, Hock searched through the manifest on the tablet in front of him. "I don't suppose you know where you're hidin' the stealth field prototypes."

The barge captain scowled back at Hock, but didn't say anything. He was, notably, not surprised to be hauling any such thing, which was promising. Heck started to sigh theatrically, then caught himself, drew himself up and puffed slightly, and said, "Captain... Sampradja, I am formally requesting you divulge information regarding the location of —"

"Enough! Bay 62. Take it and get out of here, and don't get your filthy fins on anything else."

"About that," said Liz over the radio. Hock had transmitted the manifest back to the *Wadja* so she could help search for what was needed. "62 is marked as 'Salvage, Warship, Light, Reactor, Inert'. Common enough to avoid attention, keeps prying eyes away, right?"

"Right," said Hock cautiously. "If you're going to suggest we take more innocent-sounding stuff, I don't know that we have the room." The other captain's normally expressive human face was schooled into a passive non-expression, itself somewhat promising.

"I was just gonna say that while we're here, we should grab the contents of 64 right next to it, too."

Hock flicked down the manifest on the tablet, frowning. "64 is... 'Salvage, Warship, Light, Engine, Inert.' We don't need engines, Liz."

"No, but if 62 isn't actually a reactor... trust me, Cap, we want this."

Hock noticed Captain Sampradja's face crack at the mention of Bay 64, and made up his mind. "Fine. Make sure there's room in the hold and get the grapples ready. Captain, I am formally informing you that we will be—"

The human captain snatched the tablet from Hock's fins and hit a few buttons. "Jettison contents of bay six-two; jettison contents of bay six-four. Authorization, Captain Ramesh Sampradja, Victor-Uniform-Lima-Charlie-Alpha-November. Execute."

A distant clanking sounded through the hold as two of the bays sectioned themselves off from the pressurized access. There was a hissing, then some more clanking, and finally a couple of dull thuds that were more felt than heard.

Sampradja shoved the tablet into Hock's face. The two listings, previously blue, were now a dull red. "There. Get off my ship."

Hock sank and nodded forward, imitating an ostentatious bow. "With pleasure."

* * *

The *Wadja* lumbered away from the barge, its hold stuffed with cargo containers and two more containers secured to its exterior hull.

"Barge systems are powerin' up," called Ssswoorssepp. "They should be online in another minute."

"Let's be out of range by then. Standard evasion."

"Aye, Cap'n," said Tenta. "Plotting turn-and-burns, ready to coast."

"All hands," said Liz, "brace for low power."

Hock bobbed in place thoughtfully. "Hey-hey, with luck, we won't have to rely on this evasion after this. I would have liked to get a look at it all before he popped it though."

"We put a lot of faith on that captain. He told us a number, dropped it, and told us to be on our way."

"I know, Liz. And he knows that if he didn't give us what we needed, I'll pop that insurance charge we planted and leave him sitting pretty as I turn around and blow his damn skow sky-high, all before Terran Orbital Security can get within a thousand klicks. Let it all be salvage again."

"If it helps," said Ssswoo, "I was getting some strange readings from the cargo. If it's not stealth tech, it's at least rare, expensive, and worth a fortune."

"Well that sounds promising. I'm gonna check it myself, see if we need to make another social call with the good Captain Sampradja. Liz, with me."

The captain and first mate worked their way through the

dim, emergency lit decks. The crew stood ready by their stations, braced on various hold bars.

"Prepare for burn, 1.2 seconds," whispered Tenta through the ship's intercom. "Mark." The ship jostled, then settled again, and they continued to the hold, where a few of the crew were still strapping down the new cargo.

"Hey-hey, what am I lookin' at?"

"Cargo containers, Cap'n. Four of 'em." Liz grinned.

"Where would I be without human humor?!" cried Hock dramatically, but he loved it. He floated up to inspect them. "So these boxes hold my new stealth field that the Jendeer Police Fleet used to sneak up on the Destroyers."

"Between these and the two strapped to the hull, three of 'em probably do, yeah." Liz paused as Tenta warned for, then executed, another turn-and-burn to evade pursuit.

"And the other three?"

Well, we'll just have to see when we find a place to settle in and crack 'em open." Liz grinned. "I thought you liked suspense, Cap'n."

Hock threw his fins up. "Humans!"

Liz laughed. A few of the newer crew who weren't used to it started; most species interpreted such outbursts as signs of aggression and had to unlearn it. "Fine, fine. Hock, you're here to get scraps from the Battle of Earth."

"I am indeed," Hock said as he inspected the stays that secured his cargo. "We'll be able to sneak up on any mark and take them down without them even knowing we're there."

"And what else was at the Battle of Earth?"

Hock sunk back down to Liz's level. "Liz. Elizabeth. My good Ms. Bewick. *Did you bring Destroyer scrap onto my ship?* What would we even do with it? I'm quite certain we couldn't even tell the difference between a computer terminal and a coffee machine on their ships."

"Huh. Hadn't considered that."

"That we wouldn't know how to even identify what part of an alien, omnicidal invader's ship we even had?"

"No, that we'd have Destroyer parts in the first place. There probably were some in there. But no. *Think*. What else was there? Why were the Destroyers there in the *first* place?"

Hock thought a moment, looking at the containers. Then, slowly, he puffed up and turned back to Liz, wide-eyed. "You got us—you got—you're a genius!"

Liz placed her hands on either side of him, grinning. "I know I am." She squished him slightly and affectionately, then tucked him under her left arm like an oversized beach ball. She reached her right arm up towards the containers, hand open, as if trying to grasp the sky. "Imagine the possibilities. No worrying about being spotted at Jump Ferries. We can relocate whenever we want. Think of everything we could do... with our own subspace drive."

Chapter Five

The new Alpha Point team had bonded in transit from Earth over how incredulous they all were with how little they had gotten from the jendeer. They were in the somewhat uncommon position of having fully functional equipment available to them but very little theory.

The original Alpha Point team had worked on how to reproduce the subspace drive, figuring out what materials they could replace, how well it would scale down, and so forth, but they hadn't had to concern themselves with *how* it worked. Now, the second team was tasked with inventing new disciplines of physics while having a fully functional device which reliably worked off those same disciplines.

The team had proof that it *worked*. Now they just needed to figure out what it *was*, exactly, that was working.

The leading theory was the creation of a wormhole, which would bend spacetime to make two otherwise distant points of space directly adjacent. Issues with this theory involved how to specify the end point of the wormhole from an operator at the origin point, light speed delay from the operator to the end point keeping the wormhole from connecting instantaneously over any usable distance, and the question of how mu-radiation would fit into that model.

A second theory posited that a parallel dimension existed with different laws of physics, notably a much faster speed of light, which allowed for near-instantaneous travel between points. Proponents for the "parallel-space" theory said that it could explain mu-radiation as either emissions from "p-space" or as a product of piercing the veil between dimensions. Detractors noted that even without a cap on the speed of light, time should still elapse in p-space—neither personal nor electronic records ever had any recollection of time spent between rifts—and that a ship suddenly accelerated to millions of times the speed of light would still put unbelievable g-forces on the ship and its occupants.

There was a third theory—really, this was mostly Suresh Patel with a couple others humoring him—that was called the "transporter theory". It differed from the wormhole theory by describing a breakdown of matter and supraluminal transmission to the destination rift, and didn't differ from the wormhole theory by having all of the same downsides in addition to some new ones.

To fill space on the project board, the jendeer "subspace" theory had also been included, but almost all of the team had delighted in proving it false in a myriad of ways. Within days it had been taken back down, and Eliyas Omarov slept slightly easier at night knowing he wouldn't be deleted by some buffoon with admin access to the universe.

With that out of the way, the team set about devising frameworks to test the other theories. Over the course of a week, experiments were put in motion with as many different subspace drives as possible, mostly what human-derived ones could be recovered but an aging *Fpher*-class Jump Ferry was also retired early (and reluctantly) by the JSEU to be put into use. Care was taken to only perform actual experiments on the interval, and to only do one each time, so it wouldn't become a mu-rad hot spot and draw the Destroyers back.

Fortunately, results came in quickly.

Unfortunately, they weren't the results the team would have liked.

* * *

"Nothing!" groused Dr. Morgan.

This sort of outburst was why Eliyas usually avoided the common mess areas, but the stores in his office had run out and he needed to stock up. Maybe this time he could avoid getting sucked in. He focused on grabbing as many microwaveable meals as he could reasonably carry.

"We don't have *nothing*, Iyapo, stop acting like a child."

"Well fine, Siobhan, we are getting *nowhere*. Is that better?"

"Oh, sure, much better. We're here trying to get a bite to eat in between getting discouraged by our results, and you're deciding to put your own shit on blast. We're all supremely happy for you." Siobhan pointedly stood up with her tray and brought it to a bin, grabbing the sandwich off it before dumping it, and spotted Eliyas leaving. She moved to join him; others were also leaving Dr. Morgan to vent his uncharacteristic frustration alone. On the plus side, Eliyas had avoided getting into a shouting match with the rest of the team. On the other hand, he was now in the sole company of the one person on the station that seemed to find his conversation tolerable.

"He has a point," he said, hoping to scare her away.

Siobhan scoffed. "Sure he does. He also has a chip on his shoulder because we're focusing on the wormhole theory and not his pet p-space theory."

Eliyas shrugged and the stack of meals shifted precariously. "Then he has a point about that too. Wormhole theory is the simplest and matches up with our perception of travel events but we've found no mechanism in the existing technology that enables any sort of faster-than-light signal to a remote destination, let alone enabling it to anchor the other side of a wormhole."

She replied around a bite of her sandwich. "We've been able to use it to signal a remote drive, though. Experiment series F?"

"We aren't here to build a new system from the ground up. Sure, we detected mu-rad emissions from the originating drive and the target drive, but *that's not how they are designed to work*. We're supposed to be finding out *how* they actually work before we then work on optimizing them, not coming up with entirely new and less practical methods of implementation."

Siobhan growled. "You think I don't know that? Like he said, we're running into dead ends."

"Then, Dr. Doyle, perhaps it's time to start exploring other avenues." He winced as he realized he'd made a pun, then continued on. "Maybe it's time to look into Dr. Morgan's p-space ideas."

"Oh, that's ridiculous. Even without a c speed limit it'd still take time to get up to speed then back down, you're looking at trips of months or years to go anywhere useful."

They reached Eliyas' office and he tried to catch the doorknob with his foot to open it. Siobhan focused on finishing her sandwich and let him struggle at it for a moment before he finally got it. He made for his mini fridge, sitting on the floor in what could generously be called a kitchenette. "You've spent more time chasing wormhole dead ends," he said awkwardly, as his chin was more preoccupied with keeping his food for the next few days from falling. "Can't hurt to see if the drives can access a parallel dimension. If it can't, then that's done." The boxes in his arms finally tumbled to the ground, and he started haphazardly shoving them into the freezer compartment of his fridge.

"And if it can, then what?"

"Then congratulations abound, we've proven the multiverse." He kicked the door shut; it bounced off of a box and flopped open again. Eliyas glared at the offending box of Swedish meatballs and at the lack of space inside the fridge, then picked up the box and closed the door. He cracked open a corner and popped it into the microwave on top of the fridge, hoping all the while that she'd just leave him alone.

"You know," she said, again defying his wishes, "half the reason nobody wants to work on p-space is that people don't have faith in Iyapo."

"Then everyone's as much a child as he is."

"And now you want to take it up."

"Like he said. Wormhole's getting us nowhere."

"Funny thing. If you start working on p-space, nobody will want to work on it because nobody wants to work with you."

"A level of pettiness that you, Dr. Doyle, are above, I'm sure." The microwave beeped and he pulled it out and started stirring the contents.

"You don't make it easy, that's for sure."

"You're adults. Why should I hold your hand?" He shoved the box back in the microwave. "You all act like you deserve a gold star just for being here. Well I'm sorry, you don't get *anything* until we do *something*. So leave the chocolate milk and naptime to the kindergarteners and *do some work*." He walked over to his wall console and keyed in a number. "Dr. Morgan? Are you there?"

"I'm here, Dr. Omarov. Ah, I'd like to apologize for—"

"Never mind that. You want to get started on exploring your p-space theory, yes?"

"I—yes, it's clear that nobody on the wormhole team has any plan for getting results that map onto the drive's proven operation. I know there are questions with p-space, but—"

"Yes, yes, one step at a time." The microwave beeped again and he grabbed the box from it, tenderly tossing it from one hand to the next until he got a towel underneath it. "Prove it exists, then we can figure out how to travel through it."

"Yes, exactly."

"Do you have a lab set up somewhere?"

"No, wormhole has all the lab space currently."

"Okay. We should compare notes first, then we'll start repurposing, eh, lab four."

"I'm working in lab four, Eliyas," said Siobhan from the door, which she had been leaning against the whole time.

"Dr. Doyle, didn't realize you were still here," he said in mock-surprise.

"Oh—well, if someone's there, maybe we can—"

"No, we'll take lab four. Wormhole is treading water, we'll be doing the real work. Besides." He looked pointedly at Siobhan. "I think she'll be joining our team."

She glared daggers back at him while Iyapo continued to stammer from the console. Finally, she stalked towards the other chair to take a seat. "I hate it when you're right."

"I usually am. You should be used to it. Dr. Morgan, why don't you meet us in my office, and we'll get started."

Chapter 6

Liz winced.

She didn't wince because of the loud banging that reverberated through the ship from the engine compartment. Her cabin was too far forward for it to be more than a muffled, rhythmless thud carried by a stray conduit, and it had been such a mainstay for the past few days that it wasn't anything new.

She didn't wince because of a curse shouted up the same conduit, either. A cursing crew was a happy crew. It was the quiet ones you had to watch out for, that bottled up their frustration and took it out on someone or something important.

No. She winced because Tenta was fucking Dekk again.

Liz didn't begrudge anyone their sexual proclivities. If a pilot and a gunner wanted to pass the time while the techs worked on installing the new hardware, that's fine. It even brought a certain anarchist atmosphere to the ship, which she usually enjoyed. But they did it so much, in the cabin right next to her own. *And why do kikan even fuck in the first place? They're overgrown pufferfish, they shouldn't mate like that. Drop a fucking sperm sack or something like all civilized fish.*

Not that there were any other civilized fish-analogues in known space, but Liz didn't care. She just wanted to sleep.

Liz wondered how the kikan puff instinct would interact with mating. If she threw something at the wall—say, her bunk—really hard, would the two partners balloon up immediately and bounce off of each other? She was greatly amused at the image, and quite seriously considered doing so, but eventually decided that it wouldn't be worth the upset crewmate, especially because she wouldn't be able to personally witness the event. She could rig up some sort of mechanism on a timer and walk in on them just in time to notice... but no, Liz had *no* desire to see that again. Walking in on a couple of randy kikan just *once* was enough, thank you.

Having talked herself out of it, and not having spent enough brainpower on the exercise to exhaust herself and drift off to sleep, she finally got up from her bunk to get dressed. After a particularly hard slam against the adjoining bulkhead and a clearly audible moan from Tenta, she forwent most of her gear and threw on the bare minimum of shirt, pants and boots, none of which she bothered to lace up. Getting dressed like a pirate was for when you were having fun, and she most certainly was not having fun.

She stalked out into the passageway and started walking, not particularly caring where she ended up. The crew gave her a wide berth, both because she was a predator who was walking as aggressively as one could in one-third Earth gravity (she managed it quite well) and because they could tell by now when she was angry.

Maybe *she* needed to curse a bit before she hurt someone or something.

She found herself in one of the lounges, the one with the

view outside. (Most of the *Wadja* didn't have windows; kikan shipwrights generally agreed that exterior hull space was for guns and armor.) A quick glance told her the room was empty, so she planted herself in the middle, braced her feet shoulder-width apart, inhaled, and yelled, "FFFUUU-UUUUUUUCCCKKKKK!"

She yelled quite a few things, actually. It wasn't as therapeutic as it could have been; the thicker atmosphere favored by the kikan majority of the crew meant having to work harder for a result that sounded somewhat muffled to her own ears. She made up for it by continuing for longer than she otherwise might have; then finally, out of breath, she collapsed into a nearby chair and laid her head down in her arms; maybe, if nobody said anything in the next five seconds, she might be able to fall asleep right then and there.

"Feel better?"

Fuck. Bleary-eyed, she looked up from her table, and saw the captain resting on another one in a back corner of the room. "You heard some of that?"

"Hey-hey, I heard all of it. Lotta the crew probably did too."

Liz looked at Hock for a moment, wheels turning in her head, before she dropped her head back to her arms in despair. "You've been there the whole time."

"Yep." He glanced at his comm screen. "If you're wondering, Threm won the bet on how long you'd go."

"Shit."

"You have some interesting opinions on my species' mating habits."

"Shit."

"And those of 'whatever foul god plucked them from the primordial sea and dropped them somewhere they could fuck themselves to sentience'."

"Shiiiit."

"That was my personal favorite." He floated up and worked his way toward her table. "How long has that been pent up?"

"A week or so," she said, her voice still muffled by her arms.

"Silly girl." He lightly *bomped* against her head then settled down at her table. She finally looked up at him. "I tell you to get these things out. Now you've scared the latest batch of greenhorns and we gotta calm 'em back down again."

"Sorry, Cap'n. Won't happen again."

"I sure hope it *does*, that was amazing." He paused. "Sounds like some of it has been on your mind for longer than a week."

Liz took a moment to try to recall what she'd said; without a filter, a lot had probably come from her soul straight to her mouth without stopping to bother her conscious mind on the way through. Then, she groaned again and thunked her head back into her arms. "Tell me I just told the *entire god damn ship* about my sexual frustration."

"'A dry spell longer than the Sahara,' whatever that means, yep." He scooched a bit closer to Liz. "I imagine it is *intensely* frustrating to work with this drop-dead *gorgeous* captain every day, but professional decorum prevents—" He laughed as Liz smacked him off the table, and Liz cracked a smile too.

"Do you want to know the worst part of the past few weeks?" she said, bringing her head up and staring at one of the bulkheads.

"Aside from Tenta and Dekk?"

"Yeah. That captain? Samar-something prissy-pants. Medium build, dark skin. Graceful jaw. Deep eyes. Beautiful accent." She looked Hock in the eye. "He was so *hot!* It's not *fair!* But he probably loves his moustache more than he's ever loved another human being."

"Oh, so you're saying I shouldn't try to grow one?" He flourished a bit in the air.

"Oh my *god* you would be *adorable.*" She rubbed her hands across her face, then looked back at the captain. "Uh, just so we're clear, Hock, I'm not, uh, interested..."

"Oh—oh my stars, I didn't mean—I meant for harmless and fun flirting, but if that's—"

"No, no, that's fine. I just... no offense, captain, but I'm not gonna fuck a fish."

Hock erupted into laughter again. "And me? With a mammal? Hah! No, thank you."

Liz huffed in indignation. "Well fine, guess you don't need cuddles either!"

"N-now let's not get too hasty—!"

Liz laughed, a small one that grew and grew, fueled by her exhaustion, ringing out until well after she was no longer able to gasp for air. Finally she slumped back in the chair, taking deep breaths, tears streaming from her eyes. "Whhoooooo. *Wow.* Thank you, Hock. I... really needed that." She reached for his fin and gave it a squeeze.

"Of course, Liz," he said warmly, squeezing back. He rose from the table. "And the new crew needed to hear that scary human laughter to complete their induction. Any that haven't soiled themselves by now are full share crew, they've earned it."

"And they'll be proper scared of me and do what I say, that'll be nice. Zipzi could definitely use the motivation."

"Oh, Zipzi probably shat the nearest wall ten seconds into your tirade, no way he's full share yet. But yeah, he'll listen when you tell him to clean it."

"Ugh." Liz stood and made her way back to the room's

exit. "If he's not already doing so by the time I see him he's on KP for a week."

* * *

The captain and first mate toured the ship. Hock hadn't been exaggerating about the reach her outburst had enjoyed, and Liz remembered that however much the thicker air muffled her voice, it also made it carry farther.

There was a different energy to the ship than had pervaded it the last couple of weeks; for one, about half the crew was obviously scared to death of Liz. Some thought she was going to kill them where they stood (or floated), while others simply knew that she was not in a mood to tolerate anything suspect on their part. Even Dekk caught her and apologized profusely, and said that he and Tenta'd try to be more respectful of her. (Liz didn't hold out much hope; the alternative was them taking their act to Dekk's bunk with the rest of the gunnery crew able to watch, and she didn't quite get that vibe from Tenta.)

The two-person tour finally made it back to engineering, where even over their work they had apparently heard at least snatches of Liz's ranting. When she and Hock entered the engine bay, the techs all snapped to, and Frystekh, the greasy old jendeer that kept the *Wadja* and her engineering team in shape, stepped forward. He wasn't as jumpy as most of the others, but was still standing with a bit less of a slouch than usual.

"Thought the cap'n and the, ah, human I used to call a lady would appreciate a demonstration."

"Pfah. I am too a lady."

"Ladies don't know so much 'bout shiwiik cloacas, ma'am."

Liz looked at Hock imploringly. "I didn't."

"You did."

Liz's eyes widened as her mouth set in a line in consternation, and she turned back to the engineer. "You said something about a demonstration, Fry, and it'd better be about the hardware."

"Course, o'course. Well, pluggin' it in's easy. It's human, it's all labeled and meant to be hot-swapped. Our system ain't, but there's enough common standards that we were able t' rig up some adapters."

"Yes yes yes," said Hock impatiently. "You told us you could do it two weeks ago. Why has it taken so long?"

"Adapters were done in two days. We had to spend the rest of the time moving stuff around."

"Movin—we're not in drydock, wha—whatwereyou-movingaroundonmyship?"

"Easy, Cap'n, take it easy. I know the *Wadja* better'n you do, I know what she can take. We didn't move nothin' crucial, just some life support stuff."

Hock puffed a few inches. *"Life support?"*

Fry grinned; his species was probably why human smiles were only met with mild concern from the galaxy's herbivores, while a jendeer's sabertooth rictus would make them flee in panic. "Jus' the hot water heater, our backup O2 scrubber—*backup*, I said—a couple other things. The ship wasn't in danger, you were just kinda uncomfortable for a few days."

"Fine, fine fine. So it's in?"

"Sure is." Fry ducked under some conduits to another workspace, and the others followed. In the space was a machine that looked a bit like a turbine lying on its side, strapped in with a couple of massive u-brackets. It was just under a meter in diameter and nearly three meters long, its casing a mix of original spec, damaged original spec, and missing; its most obvious feature was a red faceted crystal at the front center, pointed toward the bow of the ship. A nest of cables snaked out from it into various other workspaces and bulkheads in the area. "She's a funky little thing with weird power requirements, and next time we take a proper stop I'll have to redo all the cable management and maybe reroute a few of these conduits, but she's ready to be powered up."

"And then... off we go? Back to Trappist, or to Surkanier, or wherever, just like that?" You could almost see the stars in Hock's eyes.

"Well... not quite. See, she's got an onboard control module that the *Wadja* can talk to, but she ain't exactly got keys for her software and a pic code to grab the manual. Now, it was a prototype, so I'm gonna wager that it wasn't fully optimized, but it was human, so I'm thinkin' it can't be *that* hard." Liz dipped her head a fraction and looked at Fry reprovingly. "No offense, ma'am, I'm just sayin' that humans are good at makin' things idiot-proof."

"That's fair," Liz conceded, "we do have a lot of idiots."

"So if we can't do anything with it," Hock pressed, "what did you mean by *demonstration*? It's very pretty but I saw it while it was in the cargo containers too."

"Oh, the demonstration is for the stealth field."

"It's working? Why were you installing that when I wanted you to work on this?"

"Because I can only have three guys work on this at a time and I didn't want to let the other guys sit there doing nothing. That's what all them spacewalks were for, captain, I thought you knew."

"No, I thought they were going crazy and needed an appropriate place to let out a good yell."

"Oh, fuck, that would've been a good idea."

"Keeps things interesting, ma'am. No, they were installing the belts to the hull. Rumor is when the humans first made the thing it was a belt that a person could wear. When the jendeer military wanted to scale it up, they just made a system of multiple really big belts to wrap around the ship." Fry picked at one of his fangs, then keyed a comm button nearby. "Ssswoo, you got that drone out there?"

"Sure thing, video piping down to you now."

Fry led them back out to the central atrium of engineering. Between the door to the sector and another large conduit, a screen was mounted, which lit up with an exterior view of the *Wadja*. Liz and Hock leaned closely together toward the screen, and sure enough, noticed numerous lighter-colored bands wrapping around the sides of the ship, stern-to-bow, like lines of latitude; a few around the upper stabilizers, a band near the bottom, and two just above the central beltline of the ship. "I hate it," Hock noted.

"Me too. That's not how a dog wears pants."

"Wh—never mind. Fry, can we paint them? I want them painted."

"When they publish the specs I'll be sure to check that in the FAQ. Oh, those rumors said this can get loud, so..." He pointed to some earmuffs; Liz grabbed a pair and offered another to Hock, which he waved away and flapped his fins up to signify he could cover his hearing.

"All hands," Hock said at the screen, "prepare for stealth field test. Fry says it's gonna be loud. If your hearing's good enough that you now know more about human reproduction than you ever wanted to, then cover your ears. Wouldn't want you to get hearing damage and miss out on the next one." Liz punched him lightly in the side. "Ow. Fry, hit it."

"Aye, cap'n." He nodded to another tech who stood with two cables held apart. "We'll get ya a fancy button up on th' bridge once we got the kinks out. All hands, brace for stealth field test in five. Four. Three."

All eyes turned to the screen in anticipation. Then, the *Wadja* screamed as she blinked out of existence. The shriek felt like metal scraping on teeth dragged across a chalkboard, not in the sense of the actual acoustic experience (the sound was unholy and indescribable to the point where even trying to recount it later would prove unpleasant), but in how it felt —it set every bone and fiber of Liz's being on edge and only its middling volume allowed her to concentrate enough to look to the screen for results. Sure enough, she could see only an empty starfield—the *Wadja* was no longer visible.

An interminable second of shrieking later, the dazed junior engineer disconnected the two cable leads; the *Wadja* stopped screaming and reappeared. Liz shook away the ringing in her ears and took off the earmuffs. "Well, I'd say that was successful, Captain. You?"

She turned to her side where he had been pressed up between the screen and the conduit, but he was nowhere to be seen. She looked around, and noticed...

She started laughing. The captain and two kikan engineers had puffed in alarm at the cacophony, and bounced themselves across the room. One was trying to wriggle her way out of a cabinet, while another had just ricocheted off a couple of bulkheads and was on the floor, shaking stars from their vision.

Hock himself was stuck face-first in a cable run, his tail fin wiggling uselessly at the back of his inflated body. As her hearing returned, her laughter redoubled as, muffled against the cables, she heard, "A little help?"

Chapter Seven

"This is Dr. Iyapo Morgan, logging test P-1-3. Purpose of experiment is to test hypothesis of 'parallel-space' parallel dimension. Methodology in full is in accompanying report; for log, we are using the subspace drive from the decommissioned jendeer *Fpher*-class Jump Ferry *Salt Road*. Safety lockout regarding destination has been bypassed. Successful test should exhibit a single rift opened to p-space."

Eliyas frowned. He still hated Morgan's "p-space" term, but it seemed to be sticking among the growing team. Iyapo's theory, Eliyas' credibility, and Siobhan's vapid people-pleasing seemed to draw in those that weren't at the core of the other theories (though Siobhan would have delineated their contributions somewhat differently).

Confirming the existence of p-space was the first logical step, after which the methods of traversal could be devised. Some that joined the team likely wanted to do so just to support the testing and prove that it was impossible to open a rift to another universe, then having thus disproven the concept, to go back to their own pet theories and projects.

Still, whatever the reason, there was enough support that this test had been fast-tracked and was ready to go in just a couple of days.

Siobhan was at the terminal connected to the jendeer computer. Typically, a chip held the data for the jump, their ridiculous chip-and-display computing methods even extending to this. Instead of the usual jendeer data chip, though, Siobhan had inserted her own, with the program for the single rift opening as well as a robust set of directions for instructing the drive to bypass some of its own interlocks. (Not all of them; the test would be conducted on-interval to minimize mu-rad visibility to the Destroyers.) Eliyas grudgingly reminded himself that Siobhan's software skills were among the contributions she brought to the team.

As for Eliyas, he had prepared the sensor package to take readings coming through the rift. To calibrate the package, Experiment P-1-1 had been a control firing with a destination set and no travel and P-1-2 had been the same with a Jump Ferry transiting. The package was getting readings both in front of and behind the rift—mu-rad emissions, radio, gravitational lensing, spectroscopy, and various other methods for gathering and quantifying data. It felt overboard, but Eliyas had the budget for it and wasn't particularly in the habit of being frugal with other people's money. Maybe one of the afterthought instruments would turn up something useful. Or maybe it'd be all about the mu-rad. Who knew; that's what experiments were for, after all.

"Capacitors at full," said Siobhan. "Drive is ready to engage. Interval window opening in two minutes."

"Thank you, Siobhan," said Iyapo. "Ji-min, stand by for cutoff."

"Cutoff standing by. Expected rift stability window is... two minutes?" Kim Ji-min checked their notes. "Two minutes seven seconds without transit, after which point a rift typically self-closes. Siobhan, your package isn't going to mess with that, right?"

"We went over this, Ji-min. My package shouldn't mess with anything, but we've never opened a rift without a matching destination rift before. We don't know how it'll respond to the usual termination command."

"Right. Sorry. Nerves." They took a deep breath, then more steadily, said, "Will engage emergency cutoff if rift duration exceeds two minutes, thirty seconds, or if anyone calls for an abort. Safe word is 'abort', everybody. Cutoff standing by."

"Thanks Ji-min. One minute to interval."

"Eliyas," said Iyapo, "confirm instrument team readiness."

"Ready to start recording on instrument package," Eliyas said, turning back to his own workstation and the people seated by him. "Realtime monitoring, go/no go for your stations. Mu-rad?"

"Go."

"Radio?"

"Go."

"UV and x-ray?"

"Go."

"Gamma radiation?"

"Go."

"Dr. Morgan, all realtime monitoring is go for test."

"Thirty seconds to interval."

"Instrument package is now recording data for in-depth post-op analysis."

"Thank you Eliyas. Everybody. Here we go; Siobhan, the floor is yours."

"Copy. All stations, prepare for interval... attempting subspace rift without destination set... now."

Outside the viewports, a distant point in space, cordoned off by various beacons, began to visually distort. It pinched, twisted, then erupted open. In place of the usual bright light seen in the stable bounds of a controlled subspace rift, the light levels varied in brightness and color. Everyone stared in awe at the apparent aurora in space; after a moment, Eliyas' team regained their senses and checked their readouts.

"Getting sweeping radio modulation!"

"Mu-rad is spiking well above baseline levels."

"Supralight spectra also modulating, seeing sweeps across ultraviolet and x-ray."

"Whatever spectral shifting you're seeing seems to be stopping short of gamma rays, getting no activity in picometer scale."

"Transverse mu-rad! Confirmed, we have transverse mu-radiation!"

Eliyas was tempted to rush to their sides and see the data for himself, but he restrained himself, since he had the recording package to monitor. Iyapo had no such immediate task and rushed to the displays in his place. "Magnificent! I mean, this isn't *confirmed* p-space entry-"

"No," replied Eliyas, "But it's promising. Recording is solid."

"Hardware is holding," said Siobhan, "but I'm starting to get some feedback I don't like. Recommending experiment termination before reaching two minutes."

"Roger," said Iyapo. "Eliyas, thoughts?"

"Tempting to test how long we can keep it open but save it for the next test."

"Agreed. Siobhan, you are a go for rift closure."

"Sending termination... sent. Capacitors powering down."

"Rift is still active," said Eliyas for his team, stating what the rest of the room could plainly see.

"Sweeps increasing in frequency!"

"That thing looks *dangerously* close to stabilizing," observed Iyapo nervously. "Dr. Kim, standby for cutoff."

"Ah, Dr. Morgan, I don't know—we're not—"

"We're not keeping it open," supplied Siobhan. "Cutoff kills our power. That thing…" She nodded out the viewport, her brows creasing in worry. "That's stabilizing *itself*."

Eliyas didn't need Siobhan's eyebrows to tell him what that meant. Nobody had ever opened a rift without a matching destination—at least, not in recorded history, and suddenly his conversation with Zandkhy in his old office rushed back.

The jendeer had played with subspace, and that had set them on a path to near-total collapse. Was the Alpha Point team repeating history? Would those terrible black and red ships target this same facility again, and this time finish the job?

The screen wouldn't tell him.

"I'm losing x-ray emissions," he heard from his right, and he snapped back to the present, chastising himself for losing absolute focus.

"Roger. Speculation?"

"I'd rather not," said Eliyas, keeping his poker face. Iyapo cast him a look as though he were judging him over the rim of an invisible pair of eyeglasses, calling him out. Eliyas sighed through his nose. "It's either stabilizing itself or losing whatever energy is keeping it open."

"Maintaining the rift might tip that to stabilizing in the future."

"Noted, not needed for now."

"Right. Scopes, what are we looking like?"

"I'm losing radio frequencies. Ah… looks like intensity is decreasing as well."

"Should I send another termination signal?"

"No... ride it out." Iyapo leaned forward on the workstation before him, careful not to get in the way of its operator. He peered at the rift as the stations called in diminishing readings. The colors cycled slowly, then swirled together, the spectrum almost uniting in the bright light that characterized a normal subspace rift. Then, as though it had tried but failed, the colors dissipated, and the rift collapsed, the normal fabric of the universe healing over the wound as if nothing had ripped it open in the first place.

* * *

The next day, everybody was back in the lab going over the results. "The real question," said Iyapo, "is, how close were we to establishing a self-sustaining rift between p-space and n-space?"

"N-space?" cried Eliyas.

"The *real* question," said Siobhan, ignoring her other colleague, "is whether that was p-space on the other side. It could have been a connection to a random point in n-space with some phenomena we haven't seen before."

"Okay, first off, I'm never calling our normal spacetime universe 'n-space'." Eliyas made eye contact with the team to try to assert his will, but realized he would probably lose that fight, too. "Second off, however unlikely that possibility is, we do need to discount it. Our next logical step is sending a probe through. Someone around here must have a quick test to put together that it can run to determine the speed of light, right? That feels like a good metric to test."

"Agreed. We'll check with the team. See if they have any other ideas for what 'universal constants' might be defined differently in a different universe."

"We also..." Eliyas stopped, cursed himself for even starting to say something, then followed through. "We also should look into proper security for this site. This isn't top-secret anymore, we can have more than a token military presence."

"Are you worried about jendeer saboteurs?" asked Siobhan. Eliyas thought she might have an inkling of what he was actually concerned about, but damn her, she wanted *him* to say it.

Well, fine. If it was so uncharacteristic for him to be uneasy about the darker possibilities in play, then so much the better for convincing them it was finally time to show some concern. "No. Well... them too, perhaps. But I'm more worried about... what might come through the next time we open a rift."

Silence greeted him. Then Iyapo nodded, somberly. "You're right, Dr. Omarov. I will make sure to requisition a garrison that will... at least give us time to evacuate if we need to."

"Hey, Dr. Morgan?" Suresh said, as if reluctant to change the topic. He still had his tablet in hand, displaying the timeline of readouts from the tests.

"Yes, Suresh?" he replied, trying to change gears from Eliyas' unexpected worry.

He approached the group. "Ah, so you kept the recording package going after the test until the next interval to see if there were any residual effects. Did you see... ah, timecode T+4:14:33?"

The three frowned; Iyapo turned to his tablet, while Siobhan, who had worked in academia for a time and was used to undergrads not getting to the point, simply said, "What did you find?"

"Very faint mu-rad reading, barely above background. Seems... attenuated? Hard to tell, current state-of-the-art for mu-rad is presence, strength, and orientation. The idea of mu-rad as a spectrum is, uh, something we're possibly discovering right now. For all we know those emissions from our experiment might have been sweeping just like electromagnetic radiation was."

"Hm." Eliyas rested his elbows on his knees, steepling his fingers and leaning his chin into them. "That is definitely worth looking into. We've only encountered mu-rad in the context of subspace rifts, but it may possibly tie into the fabric of p-space in a fundamental way. We should get a sub-team on that."

"I'll head that team, if you'll have me, Dr. Morgan," said someone else.

"Of course, Dr. Hsin. Happy to have you on team p-space." Eliyas groaned.

"Anyhow," Suresh said, "this signal....? I'd like to get a pull of the jendeer mu-rad buoys to see if we can get a location. Might be good to get a record of their readings during our experiment too?"

"Fantastic, I want that. And if the readings triangulate to somewhere else, inform the Jendeer Police Fleet or whoever had jurisdiction to check it out. Could be one of our lost drives from the Battle of Earth, or..." Iyapo stopped short.

"Or the Destroyers." Suresh gulped, and Eliyas repressed a shudder. "I'm on it."

Chapter 8

"All hands, prepare for stealth field test."

This time, everyone wore earmuffs. Kikan on the crew had taken puff-blockers. Most people wrapped additional fabric around their heads.

The last few tests had gotten marginally better, but the tech had still been unbearably loud. The field was only activated for a few seconds at a time, so nobody had experienced any permanent damage, but still—everyone was being careful, even if it was just going to be momentarily uncomfortable.

Liz was back in her full pirate regalia, the yellow industrial earmuffs clashing terribly with her aesthetic. She looked at her board as various team heads reported in, then turned back to Hock in the middle of the bridge, flashing a thumbs-up. Hock nodded and keyed a button by the wrappings around his head. "Fry, everyone's good to go," came his voice quietly over the radio in her earmuffs.

"Gotcha," came the reply. "Stealth field activating in five... four... three..." Liz turned off the receiver, on the off chance it'd pick up stray interference and add one more thing to the pile of work for engineering to take care of, and braced. *Two... one...*

...

...Zero? Minus one? Minus two?

She frowned and cautiously lifted one of the cups away from her ear, but didn't hear anything past the spare shirt she'd wrapped around underneath them. "What's wrong?"

Of course, having not keyed her radio, nobody could hear her... and everybody was looking at the screen with nothing on it.

No, not nothing. Some stars.

And no *Wadja*.

She dropped the cup back onto her ear and pumped her fist upward, cheering. Looking around, she saw everyone else starting to join her. "Hey-*hey*! Success!" came Hock through the radio. Muffled cheering made it past Liz's hearing protection as she keyed her board back on.

"All hands, successful test! We are currently stealthed and also currently not going deaf!"

"Fry, great job," said Hock. "You can shut down the-"

"Captain!"

"...Yes, Ssswoo?"

"Stupid comms... I forgot... I been tryin' to call ya for a minute. We got incomin' contacts. Maybe we keep hidden, yeah?" Liz looked over at the plishken, who had removed her earmuffs but then plucked the earbud out of it to get through to those that hadn't done the same.

"What kind of contacts?" said Hock suspiciously.

"The kind that don't belong out here. We're light-minutes from anythin'. Could be brothers in piracy, could be misguided salvagers... could be system sec."

"Hey-hey, let's call it system security 'til we find otherwise. Fry, how long can we keep the field up?"

"Dunno. This is the first time it's been on longer'n five

seconds. Dunno if it burns out or anythin'. And the standoffs we installed to shut it up probably won't hold up t' hard-gee maneuvers, they were just somethin' temporary to throw plishken at the wall t' see what sticks."

"Alright. Opt—ugh. Earmuffs off, I hate these things. Fry, be ready to kill the field in case it gets loud again." Liz heard the old jendeer shouting to someone away from the comm while everybody doffed their hearing protection, and she opened a regular channel from the bridge down to engineering. Now that her ears were exposed to the *Wadja's* dense air, she could faintly hear a quiet tone at the upper limits of her hearing, the kind of tinnitus-adjacent tone that would get annoying over time but not painful.

Hock finished wiggling out of his hearing protection and said, "'Kay. Ssswoo, any details?"

"Uh, mass signature seems to be about ten, fifteen times ours. At range, can't determine number o' ships and separate classes yet."

"So no, Threm, we're not fightin' that." Threm made a show of being upset, but even he knew that fighting wasn't going to be an option. "When are they gettin' here?"

"They're pulling a deceleration burn, be here in about ten minutes."

"Okay, options. Option one: hope the field can hold out indefinitely while they snoop around, get bored, and leave."

"I thought option one was fightin'?" said Threm with a misplaced grin.

"Option one was a non-starter, Fry, where are we on option *two*?"

"That ain't gonna work, Cap," said Fry. "We can't sustain this power output for longer than..." There was some distant yelling. "Half an hour. Got some phantom power draw I can't pin down. Extra capacitors'd help but that'd have t' wait 'til we hit port."

"Okay. Fighting's out. Stealth is out. Any other options?" Liz furrowed her brow, an idea forming.

"Can we run?" asked Tenta. She held the throttle controls lightly as if to illustrate.

"Uh, not forever," said Ssswoo. "If we start running now, they've got the momentum edge and will still be on top of us as we accelerate. Could delay them, though."

"And blow our stealth cover," said Hock. "Okay. If we don't have an idea in three minutes, we can revisit that. Tick-tock, mateys."

Mateys was nearly a bridge too far, and almost broke Liz's train of thought, so she simply said, "Jump," then endured the puzzled looks from the rest of the bridge as she finished putting her thoughts back together.

Hock beat her to it. "You're not saying—"

"We jump. It's hooked up, it's getting power, hit it."

"We have no idea—we can't—we *do not know how to operate it!*" exclaimed Hock, inflating slightly despite the puff-blockers.

"Liz," said Tenta, also puffing slightly in panic, "we have, so far, powered it up three times and made it shoot its magic juice at the fabric of space, and it got weird and trippy but we have no idea how to enter a destination! Do you know how empty space is? If we jump half a light-hour in any direction but one we are days away from contact. A light-week, we're outside of this system with no idea how to get back!"

"And there's no redial button on it."

Tenta just stared at Liz. "What, tell it to do what it did last? Just follow in the footsteps of whoever brought it here in the first place? News flash, Liz, the last thing it did was poke at space without enough power to do anything!" The kikan was definitely panicking now. "This is absolutely—"

"This is irresponsible and rash." Hock looked at Liz and Tenta, his face inscrutable. Then, it started to crack.

"Oh, no—"

"I love it." Hock laughed. "I love it! How does it work, wormhole pathways? Maybe we'll just tap one of those. Come out at a jump point. Not ideal, but better than being caught here by a bunch of humans."

"Captain, you—you *can't—*"

"Objection noted, Tenta. Anyone else have *reservations?*"

Everyone on the bridge, including Liz, raised an appendage.

"Great. Now: would you rather be captured, with the rap sheets you all have?"

Over the course of about thirty seconds, every single appendage went back down.

* * *

Part of Captain Hock was disappointed that nobody was going to try to talk him down, because if he were to be fully honest with himself, he wasn't sure about the plan either.

But then, he wasn't usually in the habit of being honest, so why start now?

"Great," he said to the room still staring at him. "Fry?"

The line to engineering had been open the entire time. "I... heard that, Cap'n. Sounds like a hell of a plan. A helluva trip. Yeah. Yeah, we can do that. Get those relays on!" he yelled away from the comm. "Cap'n fancies a swim in th' unknown!"

"Fry, get me all the power you can. The last tests weren't enough."

"Aye, Cap'n. We're gonna pull the plug on the stealth field. We'll overcharge capacitors to hundred-fifty percent, hopefully that'll do it."

"Sounds good, Fry, and won't that be something fun in their reports when we just pop in out of nowhere."

"Wouldn't want 'em t' get complacent." Hock felt, more than heard, the stealth field drop.

"All hands, strap in," said Liz as she turned back to her board, eyes wide and shaking her head. What was she complaining about? She'd suggested it in the first place! Surely this was her fault. "We have unknown contacts closing on us. Presumed to be Terran Orbital Security. We are preparing to engage the subspace drive." She took a deep breath, then took the liberty of giving them the same option Hock had given his bridge crew. "Any crew member that wants to take their chances with Terran and galactic community justice at large rather than the primordial forces of the natural and unnatural universe, proceed to life raft two."

Hock just stared at her; she clearly didn't realize she'd dropped her usual "pirate" inflection while delivering the bad news. "Not that I object to giving them the choice, but I was hoping you'd try to sell it a bit better."

Liz rolled her eyes and keyed her board again, dropping out of the official voice and amending, "Anyone who jumps ship will obviously forfeit their share o' plunder for th' trip."

A couple of sharp laughs reverberated from within the ship. Hock joined them, then said, "Tenta, get us moving so we have time for the subspace drive to spin up. Ssswoo, let me know the second you get positive ID. Or actually..." he grinned. "Fovak, open a channel, pipe it to Ambassador Elizabeth Bewick's board. Surely someone so well-spoken can smooth things over with our good friends out there!"

Liz groaned while the kikan worked his own communication board. "Audio-only?" Fovak asked.

"*God,* yes." She ran her hands down her face and took off her hat, setting it on her board. She lightly slapped her cheeks a few times and sat up straight, apparently getting into character. Gone was her characteristic *lounge;* now, she was *professional.* It creeped Hock out something fierce. When she turned and nodded to Fovak to open the comm channel, her studied demeanor made her look like an entirely different human; if she hadn't still been wearing her leathers, he'd have wondered if she hadn't switched places with some strait-laced honest member of society she'd been keeping stashed beneath her console.

"Navigator Tenta, belay your previous order. We're supposed to be here." She keyed a flashing button on her board and said, with a hint of disinterest, "Incoming vessels, identify yourselves."

"Lieutenant Jacob Dinn-Jones, Terran Orbital Defense," came the immediate response. A video feed on the bridge's main viewscreen displayed a human in an understated uniform. "Identify and stand down." Hock was disappointed, hoping they'd be caught off-guard. At the same time, he noticed that this wasn't the local cops of Security; this was full-on military. He nodded to Tenta's questioning glance; they'd play this Liz's way, for now.

"This is Captain Jacklyn Sperreh, of the salvage vessel *Grey Bird.* Is there a problem, Officer?"

"You're a long way from the salvage field, *Grey Bird.*"

"If you'll take a look at our charter and contract you'll see that we have been granted a remarkable amount of leeway in our recovery operations. Fovka, in case the good officer does not have the currently operating charters ready, would you be so kind as to transmit ours to them?"

"Yes, ma'am," said Fovak, in a reasonable imitation of Liz's enunciation. Ssswoo, meanwhile, sent an image to the screen, picture-in-picture over the officer's video showing a patrol of a frigate, two corvettes and a handful of patrol boats making haste to their position.

The voice on the frigate replied, "I wasn't aware that any charter allows you to power up experimental technology, particularly in what I've been informed is an extremely careless manner."

Though she couldn't be seen, Liz still made a show of rubbing her temple. "Lieutenant Dinn-Jones, you will find that our charter has no strict prohibitions against such. That should satisfy you. We are allowed to be where we are and do what we're doing. As for the why to those... previous questions, I am afraid that this is above your pay grade."

"My rank is of no particular consequence in this matter, captain. I am afraid that I will have to detain you until your story can be verified."

And it was looking so good. "Fry, how are we looking?" asked Hock quietly into his headset.

"Ninety percent. One minute to full overcharge, Cap'n. Keep 'em talkin'."

Liz sighed. "Lieutenant, our work here is very delicate and time-sensitive. We have a timetable that we are maintaining—"

"Your timetable includes activation of subspace drive technology, off-interval? I highly doubt—"

"*Yes*, Lieutenant, in fact it *does*, and we are likely *both* in trouble now that I had to confirm that for you!" An exasperated Liz leaned forward over her board. "You let this information get out and there will be *panic* throughout Sol, *despite* the fact that we have determined our schedule in accordance with historical records and are doing so, I *might* add, far away from Earth's orbital space, thus quarantining ourselves should the Destroyers decide to make an appearance. Our timetable is meant to get experimental emission readings without the noise of the interval pulse, and our precise adherence to it helps labs throughout known space be ready to take readings. Speaking of *which*, our next test is coming up in thirty seconds, so I *advise* you to keep *back*, Lieutenant, from our vessel as we continue working with this *experimental* technology that *breaks* the laws of time and space as we know them."

For one moment—for one, drawn-out, momentary eternity—Hock thought they bought it. Then, the patrol answered, "*Grey Bird*, power down and cease all activities. Failure to do so in fifteen seconds will result in use of deadly force. Normally I'd give you a minute but you've already made your timetable clear." The lieutenant nodded off-screen, and a detachment of a half dozen fighters streaked forward toward the *Wadja*. "Next time, try to remember what captain name you go with on your forgeries."

The bridge deflated as many let out a breath they hadn't realized they'd been holding. Liz slumped, and said, "Can we transmit video to the good lieutenant, please?"

Fovak hit a few buttons, and Liz's video feed appeared on screen next to the lieutenant's. Her face showed professional disappointment, and as the officer slowly took in her garb with dawning incredulity, she said, "Very well, Lieutenant Dinn-Jones." Then, her slump turned into her customary lounge, and a smile spread across her face. "Tenta, un-belay the order. LT—can I call ya DJ? I'll call ya DJ. It's your funeral, mate." She cut off the embarrassed, sputtering officer and laughed as Tenta opened up the engines, gunning them away from their pursuers. "Hahaha! Ahhhh. Captain? You owe me."

"Certainly, and if we live to cash that in then you may consider your continued existence to be your rendered payment. Fry!"

"Hundred twenty-five for ya, hope that'll do 'er!"

"Tenta, open 'er up!"

"Seas and stars, ocean and void, protect and deliver this vessel as we *do stupid shit!*" cried Tenta, and she spun a dial and punched a button whose only label was WARNING. Space distorted in front of the *Wadja* as she accelerated and twisted to dodge shots from the pursuing patrol craft. Some that just barely missed the pirate vessel were swallowed, torn apart, unmade as they entered the distortion ahead. Hock stared at it, willing it to open into a full rift before the *Wadja* was on top of it.

The fighters caught up and loosed a volley at the pirate vessel, which Tenta just barely managed to avoid. They screamed past, spreading out to try to circle for another run.

Almost everyone stared forward at one of the fighters and, beyond it, the increasingly distorting point in space, as the *Wadja* looked to be on the losing side of a game of chicken against the natural laws of the universe. Liz alone was looking back at the captain. "If we die, I haunt you."

The rift finally tore open, the force of it shredding part of the fighter and sucking the rest through. Hock cackled. "Hey-HEY! Fair enough, Liz. *Allons-y!*"

Liz stared at Hock in bewilderment. The prismatic maelstrom reflected across his cackling face as the *Wadja* tore into the unknown.

ACT TWO

Chapter Nine

"Take it easy, you're gonna pull the rest of your hair out."

"My hair is fine, Siobhan."

"Well, pulling on it isn't helping with the headache this is giving you."

"I just—this entire time, the jendeer have had the ability to track mu-rad with equipment that ignores the speed of light." Eliyas looked up at her desperately. "Faster-than-light communication. Not dropping a data packet onto a Jump Ferry and waiting for it to propagate across jumps. Instantaneous."

"We don't know that that's how it works," she replied, massaging a growing headache of her own. "Iyapo's getting the report on their buoy construction."

"Correction," came the voice from the hallway, "Iyapo has the report on their buoy construction." He walked in and gave copies to Eliyas and Siobhan. "They're... remarkably simple. Focusing crystal of the same type as at the heart of a subspace drive, enclosure of the same rare multifunction titanium alloy they use for the rest of their subspace tech, power source—ideally radioisotope thermoelectric but the only ones still in operation today are the ones with a solar backup—"

"Wait." Siobhan flipped through the pages. "How did radioisotope fail? It's basically foolproof."

"Sure, until your radioactive material goes through a dozen half-lives and becomes inert. They haven't made them new because they haven't needed to. Hell, the radio transmitters are the most shocking durability achievement here."

Eliyas again clasped his head, staring at the floor between his feet. He slowly leaned forward and brought his elbows down to his knees to support the whole sorry affair. "My God. These things are hundreds... *thousands* of years old. They made them after their war with the Destroyers, then just... slowly forgot about them and gave up on maintaining them. And they still work."

"Dr. Omarov, can you save your assorted crises until after we've fully absorbed the report? Iyapo, continue."

"Thanks, Siobhan. The last piece of the puzzle is another crystalline structure grown in a parabolic configuration around one end of the main crystal. Since we can't exactly rely on the jendeer for any of the *how* they work, my *hypothesis* is that the current through the main crystal keeps it attuned to p-space—like putting your ear against a door—and the parabola detects any mu-rad return. Then transmit any readings the old-fashioned way." He dropped the sheaf of papers on the coffee table. "No FTL emissions or broadcasts. No mu-rad zipping around the galaxy at light-years per second. Well, not on this side, anyway."

"Right." Eliyas ran his hands over his face, then looked up. "Right. So, no revelation that the speed of light can be surpassed in n-sp—in normal space."

"Ah!" exclaimed Siobhan sharply, pointing at him.

"God—it's mind cancer, all of you saying 'n-space' for the past three days. Congratulations, you've pulled me down to your level. Fine. So nothing in the tech specs that shows any supraluminal capabilities in *our own universe.* But that could suggest that mu-rad can move faster than light in the other universe, for local buoys to be able to instantly pick up events for farther distances. We'll still have to test it, but that... feels better." He exhaled, letting out some of his tension. "Okay. So. We need... an array of probes, spread across a light-minute or two, all synchronized, emitting a predetermined burst of light and mu-rad, and a probe to collect the data. Test the probes here, calibrate for c, then we send them into p-space and see what we get."

"Now that we've been able to get a probe to remain active once crossing, yes," pondered Siobhan. "If the atomic clock needed to synchronize the array fails like the first probe did a couple days ago, we'll just get junk data."

"I also worry about opening a bunch of rifts at once so close to each other," said Iyapo quietly. He glanced at Eliyas nervously. "You know. In case it's a bigger beacon for the Destroyers."

Eliyas might have dismissed Iyapo's concerns if he hadn't shared them. "You might be right. We don't know how we accrue... heat, I suppose. Let's not find out accidentally while we're working on something else."

"Good call," Siobhan concurred. "We have data from yesterday's probe to comb through and some more experiments to devise to see exactly how the first one failed. We won't just let it rest at 'it was too advanced', we need to know what technology won't work over there, and why." She inhaled through her nose. "Can you imagine the implications if mu-rad can surpass the speed of light in p-space? Sure, the buoy system can't communicate FTL, but if we can tap into p-space and modulate mu-rad across it, boom, no more relying on Jump Ferries. And does that mean that other matter can go faster than light? What does that mean for... oh, God, for general relativity in p-space? Travel across the galaxy in days without outliving entire civilizations?"

"So many disciplines of physics we would have to entirely re-learn!" said Iyapo, perking back up.

"Or have taught to us. You know. By the Destroyers."

"Okay, Eliyas, thank you for dousing that enthusiasm."

"Don't mistake me, they're good questions, you two. I wouldn't have jotted them down if they weren't." He made a show of setting his notebook back down. "But they're good questions for later. Let's not lose focus."

"I know we're here to figure out the Destroyers and to reverse-engineer subspace technology properly," said Siobhan, "but... I didn't know how much *fun* it'd be to figure out how a whole new physical universe ticks!"

Iyapo nodded, his enthusiasm returning, and even Eliyas had to agree, saying, "It's maddening how little we knew, and it's satisfying to be cracking it open."

"Oh please," said Siobhan, "your entire existence is predicated on the ability to tell someone that they're wrong. That's why you're having such a good time, you're telling an entire species that they've been wrong about something for longer than humanity has had paper."

"I resent that you think my scientific curiosity is surpassed only by my ability to be petty."

"Petty, contrary, whatever."

"Hmph. Get out." Delivered without malice, it was still a dismissal, and the other two scientists shrugged, grabbed their papers, and left Eliyas to read through the reports in solitude.

***

"That went well," said Siobhan.

"Yeah, I expected him to flay me alive for mentioning the Destroyers."

"And you see how he didn't contradict my accusation of pettiness? The man is making progress. Why, in another five years he might match the emotional maturity of a twenty-year-old."

"How do you know Dr. Omarov?" asked Iyapo quickly, as though afraid he'd lose the nerve to ask halfway through.

Siobhan raised an eyebrow. "Normally that's a question you work up to."

Iyapo shrugged. "Small station. Figured I'd run out of hallway before I got around to it."

Siobhan laughed. "This isn't some medical drama where we discuss some big plot-shaking discovery while rapidly walking down the hall."

"You're right, and this topic is more of a 'slow discussion over untouched drinks in my cabin that affects the personal arc of the season rather than the plot of an episode' kind of thing."

"Oh, what shows are *you* watching?"

"You're deflecting, Siobhan."

"...Alright. Though I promise the drink won't be left untouched."

True to her word, five minutes later Siobhan was halfway through a glass of whiskey in Iyapo's office. His own drink was untouched as promised, but if he was more interested in dramatic tropes than his Centauri Reserve, then she wouldn't question him.

"I almost feel bad, it's not really that interesting a story to warrant all this." Iyapo just looked at her archly. "Okay, fine. I met him at MIT while we were undergrads. The kind of guy you hated to be in a class with; thankfully I only had a couple. As undergrads you see a lot of socially awkward people, students that are there because that's what you're supposed to do, taking studies seriously enough to pass but not making it their lives. He blended in with those, I guess. He was a jerk, caustic in peer review sessions—bang-on feedback but just awful at delivering it."

"Would you say his feedback helped you out?"

"It should have, but my head was too far up my own ass at first and I didn't integrate it because of how he delivered it. Only at the end of the semester was I able to look past the messenger to see the message." She took another sip. "I ran into him again as we were working on our doctorates. I don't know if he remembered me, but it was hard to miss him. By then the run-of-the-mill assholes had finished undergrad or had their master's degrees and were off to work for their family businesses or whatever, but that he was still there said something."

"That he wasn't a run-of-the-mill asshole. That he was... what, an extraordinary asshole?"

"Yes! Exactly that. Of course, various academic disciplinary actions had mellowed him out a bit—he considered the reactions that others might have to him, insofar as doing so would keep him out of reprisals. Oooh, but he knew the line he could walk, though. Absolutely infuriating man."

"I don't think he's changed much since then."

"Not as of a month ago, no. We both got our doctorates and went our separate ways. I gave him my contact info, because by that point I respected him as a scientific mind, and I'd gotten pretty decent at ignoring him as a person. He ignored me right back, I suppose—never got so much as a beat-up business card." She leaned forward and played with her now-empty glass, eyes unfocused and gazing into the distance. "I must have made an impression, though. He apparently recommended me for this project after they got him first."

"Wow. That's... an honor. Hell of a source for it, but an honor."

"No, you're right," she said, now looking at him. "Maybe he looked me up, or had my info on file, or just had someone else track me down. But I'll still take it." She paused. "I think he's softening a bit more, confined in close quarters with the team. Whether it's real empathy or just a better sense of reprisal avoidance, I can't say."

"Maybe not having the right answer first and working on somebody else's theory humbled him a bit."

"If anyone ever humbled him, there'd be hell to pay for it. And don't be so passive! It's not *somebody else's* theory, it's *yours*. Take pride in it."

Iyapo smiled weakly. "I just didn't want it to go to my head."

"Please, there's no way you could contend with the ego of Dr. Eliyas Omarov. But no, you should absolutely be proud of the work you're doing here. You didn't just have a good idea, you've followed through on it, you've put in the work to prove it and you haven't let your ego get in the way of tests cooked up to refute it." She set her glass on the table with a clink. "You're doing good work here, something career-defining. You are allowed to be proud of it."

"Well. Thank you, Siobhan, it... means a lot to hear that." He looked at her glass, awkwardly trying to figure out what to say next. "Would you like more?"

"Only if you promise to join me this time." He laughed and refilled her glass, then picked up his own. She held hers out, tilted towards him. "To work we can be proud of." Iyapo smiled, and they clinked glasses. After enjoying their drinks for a moment, Siobhan sighed. "So. What shows *do* you have around here?"

Chapter X

My name is Erudite Star of the Floral Hibernal. I am an Observer—one whose duty is to see what happens.

And my name is Stentorian Blade of Songs in Bloom. I am a Teller—one who conveys what has happened to the rest of civilization. Together, an Observer and a Teller capture a true account of anything that happens around them and disseminate it to the universe.

And my name is Porous Kin, Waking from Ignorance. I am a Recaller; for history moves in cycles, and what is new was once old, and knowing the old can help place the new in a context that is more knowable.

The three of us together make a Historian; by all concerns, a single unit that knows history, observes history, and writes history. No expedition Outside would be complete without one. Information is fast, and democratic, and distributed; but sometimes there are places beyond our easy reach, and where it might be particularly difficult to access the histories, and it is then that we are needed to help the rest of the Protectors have a complete knowledge of all.

It is common doctrine that a Historian should not be personally involved in the histories they write. We have performed our duties well, and have never before run afoul of this practice. But the history I tell today would in fact wrap us up into its threads. And moreover, more than any other history in recent memory, this history will reach new ears. And so I must start at the beginning.

* * *

Civilizations rose and fell. That is the way of things when one is unguided; peoples rise from their primordial soups, fight themselves, fight their neighbors, create grand empires or sturdy republics, but in the end they all fall.

Communication was the problem. In a universe where societies live in bubbles, they foster their own ideas, and these ideas run contrary to those of the societies around them, and they clash, and one falls. When one gets too large, they cannot stay tied together, and they fall apart, fractured from within, or easily conquered by some recent upstart.

Then, long ago, we discovered the Breath.

The Breath is woven into the fabric of all that we know; described as the voice of the universe, as background radiation reflecting off the walls of the expanding universe, even as a binding agent of life; but mostly, as the Breath. The universe is alive, and we can hear its steady respiration.

We found out how to speak into the Breath to send messages, and civilizations began to last longer. We found out how to Breathe, ourselves, to travel faster than the light of the stars; and carried by the Breath, we could travel the span between galaxies in minutes; and the pattern of civilizational collapse came to its conclusion, and cultures no longer dissolved but joined ours and wrote their own stories into its great, interconnected tapestry.

We called ourselves the Conquerors at the time, for whether by force or by statecraft, we conquered those around us. Then there was nobody to conquer; we ruled over all of space as we knew it. New civilizations rose, and we nourished them and introduced them into our midst. And we did not call ourselves anything, for what use is a label for Us when there is no Them?

Now, when we need to call ourselves anything, we call ourselves the Protectors.

Because our universe needs protecting.

As we unified, we began to notice that sometimes, in some spots, the universe did not just Breathe; it Cried out in pain. These Cries hitched the Breath, creating terrible chains stringing together the stars that made it so we could not talk across them, made it so we could not travel through them. Cries would emerge somewhere and start to spread, ever more frantic. They were temporary, momentary, but unpredictable and dangerous, and ever growing in frequency and density.

We had to forsake nearly half a galaxy to the Cries, until we learned how, in Breathing, we could cross from our universe... into another. Outside, we called it, for we had become accustomed to living Inside our own universe, with its constant Breath that did so much for us.

So we went Outside. And found that Outside, they did not have the Breath, and so would stab into our own universe out of spite, injuring it and disrupting us.

Some wanted to call them Outsiders; but for those in the galaxy that had nearly come to ruin, a galaxy that had fractured and fallen like civilizations of old, we called them Destroyers.

Outside was a harsher place to live, but as we learned to travel between universes, listening for the same Cries with which they attacked us, we followed them to their homes Outside, and brought the might of a dozen galaxies to their doorstep.

We brought peace, and our universe Breathed easy once more.

But sometimes, we heard more Cries. Coming from different galaxies, at different times. We would allow it to happen for a time, to see if it would cease, and indeed often it would. Cries, after all, were made by civilizations Outside, without the Breath to unify them, and which would fall apart in due time. And crossing Outside was taxing on our own ships and bodies. But sometimes we had to fight, to fight hard and brave to protect civilization near the Cries, to strike back against the Destroyers.

In one galaxy, the Cries started coming, as they often do. We allowed it for some time; then, as it did not abate, we went Outside to put an end to it. And the cries mostly stopped... except for a slow tempo. One that seemed deliberate; one that allowed us to conduct the necessities of civilization in a regulated and timed manner. We came to call this the Beat, and as the other Cries of this outbreak ceased, we withdrew back to our universe, and observed, and eventually civilization in that galaxy grew used to the Beat. The intensity ramped up, as more chains crossed the stars, but not the tempo—the Beat remained steady, and we decided to observe and study it. What made these Cries different? When another Cry outbreak started in another galaxy, we attempted to only suppress those that did not align with the Beat, but to no avail. Those other Destroyers had to be fully suppressed as all others had been—all but those that utilized the Beat.

In the galaxy with the Beat, civilization learned to

continue; it was almost a novelty, and certainly people were free to come and go.

But then, we noticed the Cries begin again, filling the negative space in the rhythm of the Beat.

It was localized, only in a couple of places, but we could not let it stand. We declared them Destroyers, and immediately sent an Expedition to fight them and suppress these Cries that threatened to offset the delicate balance that had been struck.

Our Expedition was lost, as sometimes happens. But the Cries stopped, and the Beat continued as it ever did.

Now, we have found that, disguised among the Beat, there are louder Cries. Not a chain between stars, but a single pinprick that Cries louder than the rest. One that has deposited small machines into space. Not the Destroyers themselves, but apparati of unknown purpose, blinking heralds of their imminent arrival.

We mobilized our fleets to be ready to respond if the Destroyers from Outside utilized this in an attack against us. We stayed well out of range while the Cries were open, and afterward destroyed the machinery so that any weaponized payload could not be deployed.

Then, these unchained Cries came from somewhere else. They were softer; and they did not hold to the Beat. Was one a diversion? What will happen through these single-source Cries, something we have never seen before?

We, the Protectors, readied a force at each. And we, the Historian, found station on the flagship of the fleet that would respond to the off-Beat Cries, the *Diurnal Sacrifice*, leading the 107th Expedition Outside.

The Admiral of the 107th, Coarse Masonry of a Shattered Well, had finished preparations among the fleet. Such preparations take time; if a fleet is not fully ready, if steps are skipped, then the hostile physics of Outside can disable a fleet for days. One of the worst times this happened, in fact, was when we first fought the Destroyers in this galaxy, in the conflict that ended with the emergence of the Beat; for a long time, the 87th Expedition Outside hung in space, brave warriors nearly torn apart by the physical laws of an alien universe, at the mercy of the Destroyers, who did nothing but watch, perchance to laugh at their misfortune.

Somehow, it always comes back to this galaxy.

History moves in cycles.

The fleet had finished its preparations; the Cries had stopped momentarily, but we were ready to set out, to breach the skin between universes, should they start up again.

Instead, something came to us.

And for the first time in history, a Destroyer was Inside.

Chapter 11

Alarms blared as the *Wadja* bucked wildly. Between ordering everyone to hold onto something and trying to get status updates, Captain Hock Corven had the time to think that this must be what it was like on the deck of an actual sailing ship in stormy seas, and considered himself fortunate to have only swum under the surface or flown above.

Mostly though, he was scared for his life and trying not to bite his own tongue.

After what seemed in the moment to be an eternity and after the fact to have been only a few seconds, the *Wadja* stopped, spit out of whatever vortex it'd been riding. The bridge lights were out, replaced by a soft violet of emergency lighting, as groans filtered through the air. Hock saw that the other kikan bridge crew had puffed slightly, and found that he'd done the same. He focused on deflating as he said, "Status, mates, call it as you can."

"All stations report in," said Liz. Blood slowly leaked from her nose, with a matching spot on the board where they must have come in contact. "Cap'n, I'll let you know crew reports as they come in."

"Navigation is fried, rebooting."

"Weapons in full shutdown. Uh, not respondin' to reboot."

"Comms restarting, getting a signal of some kind, I'll clean it up."

"Passive sensors are operational; active arrays showing major damage. Let me at least throw a camera view on the screen." Ssswoorssepp did as she said, and sent the forward camera up where everyone could see it.

She then took it back down.

"Uh, you know, we uh—"

"Ssswoo."

"We don't really, uh, we don't—"

"Ssswoo. What was that?"

"Prob—probably nothing! Just, nothing. Nebula. Who knows where we are, maybe it was some asteroids."

"Ssswoorssepp." She stopped her rapid talking and tried to grin nonchalantly to Hock, failing. "Put it back."

"Y-... Yes, Cap'n." Ssswoo swallowed and her quills shivered uncontrollably as she put the camera feed back on the screen.

In front of them was a small armada, easily ten times the force they had just escaped from. The ships were spindly affairs, their almost-familiar central cores adorned with arms, spines, and other long features Hock couldn't figure out unique names for. The ships were as black as the space behind them, with only red light coming through the windows defining their shape.

"Those are... those are Destroyers," said Threm, his fur going pale.

"Threm?" said Hock. "It is my measured assessment that you should not attempt to reboot the weapons system."

"Can we... talk to them? Has anybody talked to them?"

"I don't know, Fovak, that's kind of your thing."

"Well... transmitter is down. So that's gonna make it difficult. Receiver is definitely picking up... some sort of repeated signal. Can anyone make sense of this?"

A series of long and short tones played over the speakers in the bridge. "SOS," said Liz, stanching the blood running from her nose. "It's a distress call." She looked at the viewscreen again. "Looks like we're not the only ones that got through." She pointed to an area between a couple of ships—no, there was something there, tumbling, the remains of the fighter that had been sucked through ahead of the *Wadja*.

"When the Destroyers first came, they didn't respond to anything." Threm was still transfixed by the nightmarish warships on the screen, the old legends of his people made manifest before his eyes. "We tried for thirty days, and they just sat there... and then started slaughtering us."

"Right, so normal talking to them is out. Are they responding to that distress signal?"

"Doesn't look like," said Ssswoo. "I do see atmo venting from the cockpit. Hopefully the pilot has some kind of onboard life support because we're gonna have a hard time picking him up."

"What, the human system sec that chased us here in the first place?"

"Fovak, who knows where we are." Hock tilted side to side in thought. "We pick him up, give him a chance to join the crew, at worst he's a hostage for safe return when we're not dealing with *all of this*—" He bobbed at the mass of alien warships on the screen, his voice rising anxiously. "—so I am *once again* asking my esteemed bridge crew for *options*."

The Destroyer ships waited patiently but menacingly for the *Wadja* to come to a decision.

"Crew is reporting in, we've got injuries but nothing major." Liz turned from her board back to Hock. "The worst is Snetzk in munitions, broken leg. Doc's already on it. Uh, maybe we can just use the running lights? Some pattern repetition, prime number sequences, something like that, just enough to say, 'Hello, we don't have hostile intent.'"

"Yeah, uh—Tenta, that's your thing, yeah?"

"Yeah, I can do that. Uh, what do you want me to... blink?"

"Just..." Hock looked at Liz helplessly. "Primes?"

"Primes?" repeated Liz, shaking her head. "Yeah, they probably don't know Morse. Tenta, how many primes can you count through without thinking?"

"Ten. five. I don't know, counting's not the first thing I think to do when faced with *mortal peril,* Liz."

"Okay. Just one blink, wait a moment, then two, three, five, seven, eleven. Repeat."

"Point of order," said Ssswoo, her quills steadying slightly, "one isn't technically a prime."

Liz just stared at the plishken, then said to the pilot, "Whatever feels right, Tenta."

Everyone waited with bated breath as Tenta worked the running lights. Slowly, other systems were powered on, and as the lights came back up, the armada started closing the distance toward the *Wadja.*

"I knew I shouldn't have included the one, what does a human know about math."

"Hey!"

"Tenta, stop playing with the lights and get us out of here!"

"With *what,* Captain?" Tenta rounded on him, panic and determination mixed in her voice. "In case you haven't realized, the engines are dead. Or do you want me to get out there and vent my float bladder? There's this thing called *mass* and this ship has a lot of it! So if the order is, 'Get out there and vent,' then by the depths, Captain Corven, I want to see your dumb ass out there doing it with me!"

The only sound audible was the creaking of the *Wadja* as she adjusted, trying to relieve the stress she'd taken from the jump, as if it could relieve the stress on the bridge. Tenta looked like she didn't know whether to apologize to Hock or attack him; everyone else was considering what side they'd take and trying to gauge how the rest of the crew would align.

Hock spoke first.

"I'm... sorry, Tenta. Oh, but that is a hard thing to say! Yes. I'm sorry. This was my idea—no, sorry, Liz's—and not yours and it's not your fault, and I—oh, how do they *do* it!" He seemed to go manic, trying to play both the confidence-boosting pirate and the humble, capable leader, while Tenta had dropped all pretense in standing up to him.

"Captain..." ventured Liz, carefully. "You might want to repeat after me. 'I'm sorry for snapping, we are all under a lot of stress, but that is no excuse for poor behavior." Hock noticed that others joined him as he slowly turned to Liz as she continued her unfamiliar rhetoric. "In the future I will try to be mindful of those around me and work with them in a constructive manner to solve our problems.'"

Hock pivoted as his gaze swept between Liz, Tenta, and the rest of the crew. Finally, he said, "Yeah, what she said."

Tenta held his gaze for a moment longer, then backed down. "Alright. Keep her around, Cap'n, you're swimmin' in the dark without her."

Everyone let out a breath and returned their attention to the screens. From the largest ship, still in front of them, a smaller vessel emerged and made for the *Wadja*.

"Well," said Hock, trying to retake control of the situation. "Shall we welcome our guests?"

***

After an interminable amount of time—while one larger Destroyer ship picked up the wreckage of the human fighter, and while the *Wadja* tried to show their own incoming Destroyer shuttle where its airlock was, and both ships tried to figure out how to properly seal an umbilical between them, and the shuttle likely sampled their air to see if they could exist in it, and Ssswoo got as far as confirming that the shuttle had atmospheric pressure to begin with, and Hock informed the crew of the present situation while conveniently leaving out the altercation on the bridge, and everyone discussed how armed to be, and Hock, Liz and some boarding party crew waited with environment suits, holstered weapons and increasing agitation in the airlock—the door opened, and the pirate crew of the *Wadja* made first contact with creatures from another universe.

They were disappointingly normal.

Oh, sure, none of the figures in front of them looked exactly like any species anyone on the *Wadja* had ever encountered. They were huge, for one thing; they towered over the assembled crew, and would give most any species in known space a run for their money in the height department. Half of them were clearly the same species, an arthropod with three legs underneath and two more rising above and forward from the rear; a central thorax held oversized shoulders for the front two limbs, framing a face with three glowing eyes. No... seven? Liz couldn't tell; a face moved under a hardened open-faced helmet, one that she couldn't tell if it was part of their natural exoskeleton or something additional they wore. No mouth was visible. It was terrifying, and likely why all of the *Wadja's* crew was suddenly experiencing some variation of a fight-or-flight response.

Other species in the Destroyer delegation ranged from an almost normal-looking quadruped mammal-analogue to a bipedal tree. The only one that Liz didn't have to crane her neck to make eye contact with was a three-legged reptilian.

(Well, the five-legged nightmares also had the same eye level, but with their upper legs they took up almost twice the vertical space of a human, and were nearly twice as long tip-to-proverbial-tail as a human lying down.)

None wore environment suits of any kind as their air mixed with the *Wadja's,* so that was something; they considered the pirate ship's air breathable, so theirs would hopefully be so in return. Still, Liz felt it best to keep her own suit on until she knew for sure.

And naturally, most of the Destroyers were pointing devices at the crew that were unfamiliar in form but familiar in intent. Liz cleared her throat twice, quietly—code for, "Captain, let your ego take a backseat on this one, we don't have the advantage." (Actually, she usually just described it as, "Hock, no.")

Hock seemed to agree that his own crew, a similarly diverse cast of characters, was indeed at a disadvantage. He bobbed once in midair to acknowledge his first mate's caution, then floated forward. "I am Captain Hock Corven, captain of the fine vessel *Wadja* which you now find yourself on. Youuuu probably cannot understand me, but maybe someone's recording this, and I want to look good, yeah?"

Liz shook her head; the captain knew that she was in fact recording, and also getting ready to feed anything spoken into some first contact code that Zipzi had. (Apparently it had been bundled with other, more useful software that Zipzi had pirated. It worked on the same underlying code as a linguistics puzzle game? Liz didn't know and would worry about questioning it later.)

One of the pentapedal arthropods came forward, and a

harsh grating sound emerged from what Liz generously labeled its face.

Both sides stared at each other; the crew of the *Wadja* cast surreptitious glances at Liz as if the software could decrypt an entire language based on what was hopefully an introduction, and she noticed a few of the Destroyer crew looking towards the walking tree in what was probably the same.

Liz just sighed. This could take a while.

Chapter Twelve

The research team at Alpha Point dug into the latest stacks of data, comparing it to previous results and two weeks' worth of repeated experiments. Everyone took in the results in their own way; some had been expecting this, and others were skeptical, but the proof was there before them all.

Finally, Dr. Kim Ji-min broke the tension, looking at Iyapo. "So... Dr. Morgan. This... confirms it. You were right." It was a question as much as it was a statement.

"It doesn't matter who was right," Iyapo replied carefully. He looked at Eliyas, who glanced again at his copy of the report, then gave Iyapo a single nod. "But... we have confirmed beyond reasonable doubt that jendeer subspace drives can access a parallel dimension, one where the speed of light is not the absolute speed limit, but instead mu-radiation, which moves at a speed fast enough to cross a galaxy in... under a minute."

Everyone in the room exhaled, now that it had been spoken.

"Obviously, the scientific community will need to run

more tests," said Eliyas, staring only at his reports. The room chilled by a degree, before he continued: "But that is for other teams. For us, this is enough data to use as a working hypothesis, and we can move onto the next step. We've opened a rift to p-space. Now we have to figure out how we've been traversing it all this time."

"I think we need to see what a transit looks like from p-space."

"Agreed. Does a ship drop in and go fast to the destination, is there a bridge of some sort between the origin and destination..."

"This could loop back to the wormhole theory, with some sort of mu-rad signal to prompt the destination rift to open."

"Perhaps time passes at a drastically different rate relative to n-space."

"Can space physically be seen folding and getting distorted? If that's the case then the Destroyers would have *definite* reason to be attacking us."

"Unlikely, I can't see them surviving something like that on a regular basis and they wouldn't have left us alone for the millennia of using the interval."

"We could see a breakdown of matter for more efficient transmission of a stream of particles through p-space between-"

"Shut *up*, Suresh!" replied the cacophony of voices. And so it went; now that the tension had broken, ideas spilled forth.

Only Siobhan stayed quiet. Eliyas noticed. "Dr. Doyle. What are we missing?"

The room stilled again. Without looking up, Siobhan asked, "What is happening to our probes?"

There was no answer. She continued, "Our tests have shown p-space to be similar enough that the probes we're sending should survive for some period of time, but they're never present by the next interval. The latest tests haven't had broad-spectrum equipment but they should still show *something*. Instead, it's just empty."

Eliyas tilted his head, then looked back to the report. "Where are you looking?"

"Page sixty-seven, test P-3-4, and... page fifty-two, P-3-5." People shuffled through electronic documents or sheafs of paper. "P-3-4's pulse timing was offset from the rest, and neither it nor three-five read any extra pulses. So the emitters didn't last longer than six hours, which is... incredibly unlikely, with how simply we built them."

Nobody wanted to say what everybody thought. Except for Eliyas, who didn't care what everybody thought: "You think the Destroyers are... destroying... the probes."

"Possibly." She shifted her weight and finally looked up. "It's also possible that p-space and n-space don't have a 1:1 spatial correlation, and they've drifted by... light minutes, hours, light years, depending on the relative speeds of the universes."

"Unlikely," said Ji-min. "The first probe tests where we had it reporting back through a portal we kept open showed it keeping station without any outside forces acting on it. If a portal kept a part of p-space from moving while everything else was, that would be... some sort of catastrophic destruction of space-time that I don't want to contemplate until we've Occam's Razored everything else out. If the universe is moving, the probes are injected into p-space with momentum such that they should still be stationary from our point of view." They stopped and looked at Siobhan. "Something outside of natural causes is removing our probes."

After a moment in which everybody was considering

alternatives, Dr. Ames Mallway said softly, "Is this a first contact situation?"

"This is hardly our first contact with the Destroyers," scoffed Eliyas.

"No, but I mean... we are on their turf now. They're probably *right there*. Which, by the way, means we should be *very* careful with anything else we send through." He took a deep breath. "This is probably time for a diplomat to show up."

"Good. Diplomacy's never been my forte," said Eliyas.

"You don't say."

"We don't even know if we can make the return trip," interjected Iyapo to keep Eliyas from responding to Siobhan. "We don't want to send someone into p-space to encounter them on their home turf, after all historical attempts at communication with them failed."

"Millennia ago!" said Ames, getting louder. "The jendeer have no idea how their own subspace technology works, they probably screwed up first contact attempts too. Look, I'm not saying we send someone on a one-way trip, but open a rift and send a signal."

"Fine!" Eliyas said, matching Ames' volume. "And how do you propose we do that?"

"Enough," said Iyapo. He stared Eliyas and Ames down until they backed off from their impending shouting match. "Ames is right, we need to devise some sort of communication method, otherwise there won't be anything for the diplomats to *do*. Suresh, any luck on your mu-rad spectrum analysis?"

"Ah—no, not really. We've figured out how to use some drive components to send a mu-rad signal without the full power draw a drive normally takes, but any sort of tuning or anything is still beyond us."

"A wideband digital signal is better than nothing," said

Siobhan. "Build us a transmitter and the software that can easily take messages on the fly and convert it to an obviously manufactured signal that we can broadcast over the noise that the rift makes."

"On it."

"Ji-min, you and I are going to look through records to figure out what we can send with a digital signal. We'll look at 20th century human SETI, and reference what other species' have done too, see what's worked and what hasn't."

"Sure thing."

"Ames, you brought up the idea of getting some professional diplomats here, so why don't you send a message back to the home systems on the next interval and get them to assemble a first contact team. We need a human on that team, then whoever else is also qualified."

"First contact on behalf of humanity, then?"

"Of this *universe*, Dr. Mallway." Eliyas stood up. He looked like he wanted to apologize for shouting at Ames, which was about the closest thing one would get to an apology from him, and Ames seemed to accept it. "The Destroyers present us with a united front, and we must do the same to them. We are not one government here, but we cooperate well enough. Get all of the big players to send an envoy to the team, they can figure it out from there." He made eye contact with each team member present. "Until they arrive, I recommend we open no further standalone rifts. We must act as if the Destroyers are on our doorstep.

"I will also impress upon the home systems that the patrol fleets we've gotten so far are not *enough*. They weren't enough last time and they won't be this time, we need an actual military armada in case the Destroyers decide not to wait for further action on our part." Eliyas kept his gaze steady, but Iyapo knew that he too was occasionally haunted by the prospect of an invading fleet storming through rifts, making Alpha Point their beachhead—again.

Iyapo made himself break this latest silence. "While we're stuck on this side, I want everyone to work on theory, equipment design, something. When we're good to open up rifts to p-space again, I want us to hit the ground running. Ames, I'll send that message for a first contact team, I want you to work with Suresh on mu-rad spectrum analysis, tuning, modulation, anything that can confirm mu-rad's use as a signal carrier."

"Got it."

"I'm also going to get the latest from the Destroyer salvage team. Last I heard it's all pretty standard construction—at least, nothing stranger than in the subspace drives. I'll send them our own data and we'll see if anything shakes out. Let me know if any brainstorms hit you about that." Iyapo surveyed the room, suddenly self-conscious of how he'd taken charge—he had originally played third or fourth fiddle when the team had first assembled. Before he could slip and let anything show, he nodded and wrapped things up. "Thank you, everyone. Let's use our time wisely."

He sat back down—when had he stood up, exactly?—and scrolled through his tablet, more out of needing to fidget than to look for anything. After a moment, he grabbed a stylus and started writing the team's to-do list to the project board, as others dispersed through the room and out into the rest of the station. He stole glances at the team; they all seemed to take his word for how to proceed. Siobhan gave him a smile as she left and everyone else moved to other areas. Only Eliyas stuck around, not approaching but not leaving either.

"Any more thoughts, Dr. Omarov?" he prodded.

Eliyas waited another moment, then, as if shrugging aside a mountain that had fallen on him, said seven short words.

"You're doing a good job, Dr. Morgan."

With that, he left the room. Iyapo discreetly pinched his leg and, satisfied that all other signs pointed to him still inhabiting the real world, got to writing his reports and letters.

Chapter XIII

We realized rather quickly that these Destroyers were not an invasion force. Soon after that, we ascertained that neither were they any sort of envoy.

They were, as we came to learn as we built a common lexicon, fools.

"They insist that they are merchants," said Erasure of Grass in the Moonlight. She and the other captains of the 107th Expedition Outside were gathered at a table on the *Diurnal Sacrifice*, one with Coarse Masonry of a Shattered Well at its head.

"Setting aside the claims to the contrary by this Lieutenant San Martín, how do you explain the weaponry?" asked the Admiral.

"The Destroyers are savages," replied Erasure. "Likely among themselves most of all. Any merchant must defend itself."

"From what?" asked Coarse Masonry. "From pirates. That is what these are—pirates who decided to come Inside to open up a new revenue stream. I see no reason not to take this San Martín at his word."

"If they are pirates then they are idiots." Nobody at the table disagreed with Erasure's statement. "They are stupid and stubborn, and we have wasted far too much time on them already."

"We are still learning much from them," said Winding Drop of Thunder, Captured. "Their language, for one. And they are so inexperienced in matters diplomatic that they do not realize what they give away when they speak of how their travel works."

"And you believe what they tell you?" asked Erasure. "I thought it took more wits to be a captain of this Expedition."

"Enough." Coarse Masonry looked at each of his captains, then to Stentorian Blade of Songs in Bloom, who had been standing to the side. "And what does the Historian think?"

Historians rarely play an active role in any matters. We observe, and we recall, and we tell. However, Erudite Star of the Floral Hibernal had found herself to be a favorite among the newcomers. They had apparently never met a plantoid sapient species, and her early role of serving as a translator of their words meant that she often worked closely with the Destroyer called Liz, who performed the same role for them. She enjoyed the time she spent with them—at a professional detachment, of course—and fostered that enjoyment to try to pry from them what secrets she could.

It helped that they were all so small, especially the floating ones. We found them to be rather adorable.

I thought for a moment before the gathered captains. Though Erudite Star is our Observer, our trichotomy often lets us observe from multiple places at once, but the captains also knew of the Destroyers' fondness of us, and there is a reason that I, our Teller, was in the room.

"I believe," I said after another moment, "that despite the convictions of their captain, they do not know how their travel works, in a scientific sense. But I do believe them when they speak of how it works in a social sense."

The Admiral flared his eyes at me in suspicion. "Explain."

I shifted my weight back to my hind leg. "Whether they are merchants or pirates, their profession lends them a professional knowledge of how commerce is conducted. This knowledge permeates them, so when they speak of travel limitations in their universe, they are stated as a matter of fact, not in order to convince us. I offer, for example, a word we learned today: 'Efteeell'."

One of the captains waved one of his upper legs. "And this 'efteeell' is?"

"An abbreviation of a term, 'faster than light'. However, this term is always used in this fashion, with no variations. If they had made up a story about their universal laws revolving around the speed of light as a universal constant that spacetime cannot exceed, then we might expect them to refer to attempts to surpass it as, yes, faster than light; but also quicker than light, or light breaking, or any other linguistic expression. 'Faster than light', though three words, is used as one word, and not one that would have occurred to anyone Inside because for us, the speed of light is no more a barrier than the speed of sound."

"And what about this... 'radio'?" asked the Admiral.

"They use 'radio' in the same way; when pressed, they reveal that it is a way to use light to communicate, but their everyday perception of it is different." I paused. "We feel that this lends more credence to the theory that the speed of light is the fastest force in their universe, as communications would be performed with the fastest means available. For them, that is light, and this 'radio' part of it that is so commonplace that for the layperson it is divorced from the concept of light itself."

Everyone pondered this as I resettled my weight and again sank back into the corner. They argued more, and drafted a report to send to the 106th Expedition Outside, waiting by the site of the other Cries, which had been silent for the latest span of time. When the meeting finally finished, I departed to meet up with the rest of the Historian.

* * *

"You seem tired," I said, as Stentorian Blade returned to our quarters from his meeting with the Captaincy.

He said nothing, but climbed into the hammock with Porous Kin and myself. Stentorian Blade's five limbs completed the embrace in a way that those of Porous Kin and myself never could, though technically we each only had one fewer. (My branches do not count as limbs, no matter how much Stentorian Blade may attempt to reassure me otherwise.)

Porous Kin let out a deep, grinding rumble to welcome Stentorian Blade and folded one of their obsidian-like arms around him. We lay there for a time, all internally processing what we had done throughout the day, not hurrying; the business of being a Historian would happen when our mental states were ready.

"I do not think they like us," said Stentorian Blade first.

"I would think not. According to them, we nearly eradicated them." Porous Kin rumbled in agreement.

"No, I mean, those of us descended from the Conquerors." Stentorian Blade shifted a little and I lifted my head to free his leg for him to gesture with. "Though they differ in form, and seem to come from different biospheres, they are all animal-analogues. I would think that would engender familiarity with us, but... I feel as though I do not want to translate this 'bug' word. But they consider plantoid sapients to be a rarity, and are entirely unfamiliar with lithoid species at all—where they are from, a rock is a geological feature and nothing else."

"Give them time," Porous Kin intoned. "If they move as slow as they say, they have only their galaxy. It took a long time for you to find us."

Stentorian Blade conceded the point, though it was not what he had been working towards. "I only mean to say that your novelty is likely what keeps them speaking. Everyone else on this ship is either a descendent of the Conquerors or they are another animaloid species."

Porous Kin rumbled in dismay. I turned to them and said, "I understand, but we do what we must. We are the Historian and will serve as such until we are recalled. I noted our peculiar situation to the College and advised that another Historian should perhaps be sent so that we might focus on our unexpected roles, but have heard no reply." Porous Kin rumbled again. "Don't speak that way of the College of History," I admonished him. "It is because of them that we were brought together."

"An act of good does not nullify an act of negligence," said Stentorian Blade, recommitting to the embrace.

"Wise words, Elder."

"We are the same age, Erudite Star."

"But my species lives longer. I am but a child." Porous Kin rumbled in agreement.

"You two cannot keep using that against me," said Stentorian Blade with exasperation, but without conviction. It was a well-trodden joke between us.

We again settled into comfortable silence, and eventually fell to slumber in each others' limbs.

* * *

I do not like speaking.

I do not like discovering the unknown.

I like learning what is known, and applying it.

That is why I am the Recaller.

But I also fulfill my duty.

Stentorian Blade believes the Destroyers respond better to non-animaloid species.

Today, it is my duty to find out.

Erudite Star and I met with the small invaders.

I like the floating ones best. They become a sphere when frightened, one I can hold in the palm of my hand. Their spines do not bother my igneous flesh.

I also like the fluffy bipeds with large teeth. I allowed one to bite me. It was curious about my flesh. We learned a new curse word.

Erudite Star worked with the endoskeletal biped with the smooth covering, named Liz. They continued to bridge language, though we had working communication already.

I merely answered questions about us.

Prevailing theory is that they are pirates, not diplomats.

This makes sense. Diplomats would be more curious. Only a few of them have interest in our history and what it means to live Inside.

The Breath interests some of them, but they do not have the technical knowledge to understand, or the societal knowledge to care.

I asked one of them, why do you like me more than Stentorian Blade? I am larger. Harder.

They said they do not know. The image of those descended from the Conquerors seems to trigger a universal fear response in them.

Exoskeletal beings are not unheard of for them—they gave us species names that mean nothing to us—but the form of the majority species Inside is somehow more frightful.

When I asked if they knew of any other attempts to come Inside, they again begged ignorance.

Ignorance is easy to assume from them. They are small. But we cannot be tricked.

Still. If what they say is true, their galaxy is the only one they have known, and they alone have engineered the Beat.

We cannot say what that means. But even if the ones before us are foolish, it would be a mistake to generalize them all as such.

As we finished for the day, and left their holding area to see to our other duties, Captain Erasure of Grass in the Moonlight intercepted us.

She told us that the other source of the Cries, which had lain silent for more than half of the time we were learning from our captive Destroyers, had again shown activity—and perhaps an intentional attempt at contact.

We were to rendezvous with the 106th Expedition Outside, a voyage that would take us time.

But the contact protocol looked familiar. So we would commune with the 106th during the voyage.

And maybe by introducing our captives to any new Destroyers, we would learn more from their unscripted, surprised interactions.

Before this, we had begun to feel that we had learned what we needed from them, and they were not needed on the Expedition fleet.

We were getting ready to send them to a planet they could be held at and studied more closely, by those more qualified than I.

But it seems history had more in store for us.

Chapter 14

The past month had been an exercise in dissociation for Hock Corven. He had been an entrepreneur, a successful one, able to provide for himself and his employees. He had seen an opportunity to grow his business and give himself a competitive edge. He had had a natural distrust of authority and valued his own independence above all else.

Now, he was talking to a walking tree, a giant bipedal golem, a bunch of big bugs and a menagerie of other unfamiliar beings. He was a charismatic leader who now found himself in the uncomfortable position of negotiating with captors who held all the power to keep his friends safe. ("Crew", as a word, was flexible enough in many languages to cover both "employees" and "friends", but the intention behind the word had changed.) He was trying to manage the flow of information to keep from giving away too much to the Destroyers while coming to grips with the fact that *they were currently in a different universe,* so what even counted as valuable intel?

That was what he had the hardest time coming to grips with. When he had given the order to open the subspace rift to escape the Terran patrol, he had been prepared to end up in the middle of nowhere, or die, or potentially end up somewhere near civilization (the last one on only an incredibly slim chance). Ending up in the lap of the Destroyers had occupied the barest sliver of possibility in his mind—known, maybe, but not consciously acknowledged. And that being in another *universe?!* It was too much to handle.

Still. He tried, he worked to keep his crew's spirits up, and he leaned on their captors to make sure that everyone's needs were met as best as possible.

Almost no one in the crew was suffering any ill effects from the alien physics. *Almost*—Polyth, the ziggern'th on the crew, was down for the count. She'd started complaining of migraines after a couple of days and it got worse from there. Ziggern'th were lightly telepathic among their own species, and the ship's medic theorized that something about the physics in this universe was causing a biological short-circuit in that part of her brain. (Or she'd had an ill-timed aneurysm. Something about a sample size of one.)

Hock and the crew were able to stay on the *Wadja* when they weren't on the Destroyer ships for various interrogations-by-any-other-name. The pirate vessel was secured to the Destroyer hull, so they were unable to fly away, and besides, the *Wadja* was still undergoing testing and repairs from the rift transit, and even if they could have gotten free, they would have had no idea where to go and how to get there. Their best bet was waiting for an opportunity to make it back home.

Whatever the universe—or definition of "crew"—deep inside, Hock Corven was still a pirate captain. He was always on the lookout for opportunity.

Case in point: Lieutenant Carlos San Martín, formerly (potentially) of Terran Orbital Defense. Having another human on board seemed to help with Liz's morale, and having a new crewmember gave something less alien for the rest of the crew to focus on.

Trust wasn't immediate, of course, no matter how attractive he apparently was. (Very. Liz made sure to stress this to Hock—*very*.) Hock had her give him a limited tour of the *Wadja* that left out some of the more hidden smuggling compartments, and didn't mention the stealth field generator. There was a possibility he wasn't told about it by those up the TOD command chain, as he'd only been sortied after the *Wadja* had powered down the stealth field to divert power to the subspace drive. So Hock tried to keep such things away from the pilot until he'd proven himself as fellow crew, and not just a convenient point of familiarity.

Not that it was that big a deal, at the moment; the stealth field wasn't working, and the nearest authority who would care about it was literally a whole universe away, and without knowing how to get back where they'd come from, Hock didn't want to use the (also presently nonfunctional) subspace drive for fear of going to yet *another* universe instead.

So Hock drifted around the *Wadja*, kept an eye on Carlos, and met with the Destroyer Historian trio regularly. And then, finally, opportunity came knocking.

* * *

Liz was very glad to have another human on board. She'd always viewed her crew as family (with all the ups and downs a particularly tumultuous family tree might endure), but with all the unfamiliarity that had been thrust upon her in the past month, making the acquaintance of Lieutenant Carlos San Martín had been nearly delightful.

"Oh, what's that, you always knew you wanted to be a

fighter pilot, so you studied hard in school and went to the academy but almost lost it all because of an irresponsible roommate, but earned your place in a story that would make a good popcorn movie? Well, I had no idea what I wanted out of life, went to school because my parents wanted me to, got a corporate job because that's what you were supposed to do, then fell madly in love with the lawless lifestyle when the ship I was on was boarded by Captain Corven on his very first score after parting ways with his predecessor, so I joined onto their crew and haven't looked back since. We're friends now!"

When faced with the reality of aliens from a *different universe* on one side and the pirates he'd been ordered to gun down on the other, Carlos barely hesitated a second, pulled the Terran Orbital Defense patches from his flight suit, and asked when he might be able to get some leather pants of his own.

In Liz's estimation, he would look *very* good in leather pants. His flight suit was merely acceptable; and as nobody else had any clothes that would fit a human frame right, after a couple weeks, Liz invited Carlos to her cabin where he didn't have to wear it.

Tenta alone earned the right to comment on the arrangement. Everyone else, Liz advised to kindly fuck off.

One morning, after having woken up and enjoyed each other's company, they lay together in Liz's bunk, and Carlos asked, "Have you ever slept with a xeno?"

Liz punched him in the shoulder, playfully but not lightly. As he rubbed his arm with a soft "ow", she said, "Okay, first off, rude, just say non-human. Second off, rude, you don't just *ask* a lady who she's slept with before until... I dunno, a couple months in?"

"Lady, eh? Ladies don't know how to do that with their

—" She punched him again. "Alright, sorry. Just... wondering how close the crew is, I guess?"

"Hell of a way to ask. Tenta and Dekk had a thing goin' while we were workin' on the subspace drive, but they more or less got over each other shortly after we got here. Last year we had a coupla randy shiwiik, that was *loud*, ended up leavin' port without 'em. Don't think they realized. Aside from that... no, not really a thing."

"Oh, so you and the captain...?"

Liz glared at him and he quickly pulled his shoulder away, covering it with his other hand. "For your information, Captain Corven and I have a physically platonic relationship that, let me make clear, is *none of your business.* Understand?"

"Yes! Sorry. I—I went too far. You all like to live up to the old pirate movie thing, and it's, you know, not my speed but I figured I'd see how far those things went."

"Carlos, the pirate crews of old weren't just seafaring orgies. You're thinking of 'a lover in every port'."

"Ohhh." He nodded, then looked back at her with that damn twinkle in his eye. "So, how many ports have you—"

* * *

Hock was just about to knock on Liz's cabin door, figuring she and Carlos were about finished, when he heard a loud yell of pain from inside. He considered turning right around and meeting with the Destroyers without her, but ultimately just cleared his throat, knocked on her door, and said, "Did I come at a bad time?"

"We were just finishing up," called Liz from inside. "Give me a minute."

Moments later, she emerged from her cabin, still lacing up her bodice. Carlos sheepishly waved at Hock, halfway into his flight suit. How he managed to take longer putting on a one-piece garment when Liz strutted out wearing a full wardrobe, Hock didn't know. "Hi, Captain," said Carlos sheepishly.

Hock wished he had an eyebrow to raise, but settled for an acknowledging, "Mr. San Martín," and set out.

"Human men are assholes," explained Liz to a question Hock didn't ask, as he led her through the ship toward the airlock, and the Destroyer warship semi-permanently attached to it.

"Oh? Does that bring an end to Mr. San Martín's living arrangements, then?"

"Depends on how well he learns. If he shuts up and does what he's told, he'll make a good crewmember."

"And a good mate? Is that how you like—"

"Cap'n, I've got plenty of ammo left in my fists, if y'wanna try me."

"Oh, nonono, just... didn't know if that's what you're into."

Liz just glared as Hock slipped on an anti-grav harness. The Destroyers preferred a thinner atmosphere, like most species back home, and even heavier gravity, exceeding even Earth's by a small fraction. He idly wondered if there were any floating species in this universe, and how they handled the environmental conditions of the apparently-dominant species.

When he was ready, they headed down the umbilical into the warship and, under the watchful eye of some guards, to what the crew referred to as "the playroom". The playroom was a communal area where the cultures could learn about each other, converse, and generally have unstructured time to exist together; the fact that the ceilings were so tall added to the idea that the crew of the *Wadja* were children in a preschool, trying to impress the adults, something Hock tried very hard to put out of his mind whenever he floated in.

Only one Destroyer waited for them in the playroom—the one that looked like a tree, whose name was long and esoteric but one element translated to "Star". The golem and the bug that hung out with her (Kin and Blade) weren't there at the time, and most of the *Wadja's* crew had tired of the novelty and the perceived condescension, so the three of them were the only ones present. Star was sitting at one of the tables, and said, "Welcome, friends."

Liz climbed up one of the chairs (something that clearly didn't help dispel the infantilizing nature of the surroundings), while Hock just floated up and, rather than returning the pleasantry, said, "We are moving."

"We are seated. Why say we are moving?" replied Star.

"Ship is moving," Hock clarified, secretly pleased for once that the simplified form of speech they were using lent the sort of patronization into his voice that comes with talking to a child who can't speak correctly. It truly was the little things. "Air... feels different."

"Sounds different," added Liz. "Floor vibrating different."

The tree stood up a bit straighter, something that Hock had noticed she did when thinking something over. "Yes. Moving. Might have... thing to do."

"Task," said Liz, adding another word to the Destroyers' growing vocabulary. Everyone was talking in the common Trade language (well, common to the home universe, anyhow). Between the software that helped establish linguistic baselines and the tree seeming rather adept at languages, it was just easier to use the one tongue. Few in the crew knew more than Trade and whatever their native language was, if there was even a difference. Hock only knew

Trade, but had such mastery over it that it usually pained him to be so curt.

"Task? Okay. We might have task for you."

Hock rubbed his fins together. "I'm listening."

* * *

"You met with the Admiral?"

"Oh, yes, charming creepy bug thing, great guy or girl or something else. Their enjoyment working with someone a tenth their size was absolutely palpable, some things transcend all barriers."

"Really?" continued Zipzi.

Liz smacked him on the back of the head as though she could teach him about sarcasm through sheer percussive force. His head bobbed far on his long neck as Hock ignored him and continued, "The important part is: we are going on a diplomatic mission! Hey-hey, look at us, all respectable!"

"What do you mean, diplomatic mission," asked Liz, narrowing her eyes. She was probably regretting not accompanying Hock to the briefing, but Star had had some other request for her, something about food testing. He'd stopped paying attention when he'd left the playroom.

"Well. They can tell when we jump, right? The 'chains' or whatever. And they can also tell when someone tries to open a rift without a destination. Or I guess that just makes this universe the destination. So it turns out there's another place that's happening that they weren't telling us about. Surprise! I'm sure it just slipped their minds.

"So this area hasn't been active since we got here, but just started back up. And apparently they would like us to be their delegation to pop on over and tell the folks back home how grand they all are." Hock spun a little ascending circle in the air. "Really, that tree person has learned so much that I don't know why they don't just stuff us in a deep dark hole somewhere and send their diplomats in on another ship, maybe they're worried it'd get shot down. Which it would."

"Wouldn't we... y'know, also get shot down?" asked Threm.

"Well, I'm told that they think whoever's opening the latest set of rifts wants to talk. They got a signal. A prime sequence! Starting with two." Tenta groaned as Hock continued. "So they're expecting someone to come back. And as to whether they would want *us* dead... depends where we're going. I'm told it'll take two days to get there. We don't know how fast they are—they don't have the speed of light to slow them down, but they also don't have subspace jumps. They're, uh, kind of already in subspace. They can't well do a nice instantaneous jump through our universe the way we can through theirs, right? Ha—okay no that's probably terrifying and they've probably gotten the idea and oh no I hope that doesn't seriously mess things up." He floated still for a moment as the crew just stared at him, then shook himself, attempting to dismiss the concern like a canine shedding water, and continued, "Well if it messes up everyone else, then it's a good thing for us. So! We have some preparations to make. Fry, how's my girl?"

"All electronics are patched together. A couple of 'em don't take kindly to the physics over here so I've put 'em on cutout circuits, we can loop 'em back in when we're back home. I think I've figured out an efficiency issue with th' stealth field, should run for longer, but I haven't tested either of our newest systems yet, haven't had th' chance."

"Be a dear and do that for me, I want to be ready for anything." He clapped his fins. "We're being sent by the Destroyers to talk to some stuffy diplomat and nobody in this equation particularly cares for us, so we're gonna watch out for each other. That includes the *Wadja*—get her in tip-top shape and she'll take care of us right back. Any questions?" Nobody responded. "Marvelous! Let's get to work."

* * *

At the end of the next day, Hock had just finished touring the *Wadja* with Liz. Things felt more right than they had at any time in the past month. The ship was alive and with purpose. Even Carlos was pulling his weight, slotting into the crew where he was needed and working just as hard.

"So that's the ship in order," said Hock. "How's the crew?"

"Everyone's excited to get moving again. There were some questions about the passage of time, if it's been a month, or if it's somehow been a day or a century back home while we've been here. I told them I figured out this Beat thing to be pretty close to the interval, we've gained or lost a day, two at most, if anything. Most are just glad we're going back to our home universe. Poylth was awake for a few minutes today, she was so happy when I told her that she passed back out." Liz grimaced. "I don't know how much longer she can last here."

"If all goes well we won't have to find out. Any other problems?"

"Uh, let's see. Remember how Hel'kef was worried that his soul might not have come through the rift with us?" Hock groaned quietly. "Now he's worried that if we go back it might not be able to find him. I told him, it seems like subspace jumps always come through here, so just think of it like a jump that's taking a long time. He seemed to take that well. Didn't have the heart to tell him that if a rift can separate you from your soul then we've all been vampires for decades."

There was a crash as equipment fell in a cabin they were passing. Liz glanced in and swore, and sped up walking.

"Well now that you've told him. Anything else?"

"Nothing else with the crew. I still find your plan a bit light on details."

"Liz!" Hock clapped her on the shoulder and they stopped in front of the airlock. "We were born into this universe without a plan and I will damn well make sure we leave it the same way." Liz just rolled her eyes. "Everything will be fine. It's simple—what could go wrong? They release the clamps, we just fly out on our merry little way, and—"

The airlock chimed with a connection request. Hock cleared his throat, dodged a look from Liz blaming him for tempting fate, and hit the panel. The door irised open, and Star stood stooped on the other side. Kin and Blade were behind her.

"Uh, hello there, friends! How can we, uh, help you?"

"Where we staying?" asked Star. She began to step through the airlock, and Hock realized in horror that each of the three had a bag of what was obviously light luggage with them.

"Captain. You never told me to expect guests."

"I, ah, I was not expecting guests!" Hock played through the briefing with the Admiral in his mind. "Must have been a translation slip-up along the way. Well, uh, theee... *car*-go bay, of course! Not our best looking place by any means, I wish I could put you in an observation lounge, but I'm afraid Kin would tear my ship apart on the way." The golem was twice Liz's height and three times as wide; if Hock tried taking him through the *Wadja's* cramped passageways he'd look like some fool of an action hero crawling through air ducts.

The Destroyers talked amongst themselves for a moment. Then Blade said, "Show me where is cargo bay. They will stay and wait."

"Are you sure, big guy? I can pop the door and you can all spacewalk to it from outside, it's—"

Blade stepped forward, his bulk filling the passageway, his five legs braced against the circumference of the wall. Hock puffed a bit in alarm. "Will be fine. Please go. I follow."

Hock gulped and forced himself to deflate. Before he led the large pentaped through his ship, Liz caught Hock's eye with another glare. "This doesn't change anything, does it, Captain?"

"No! Nonono, of course not. The plan is... exactly the same." He smiled for the Destroyers. "Nothing has changed, except now that we have some guests to make things more... exciting. If you'll follow me?" He spun and led Blade down the passageway, imagining all the ways the plan could fall apart.

Chapter Fifteen

"Rift is open and stable."

"Thank you, Dr. Doyle. Dr. Omarov, are we ready to receive?"

Eliyas had taken the mu-rad detection station himself and checked the signal. "Mu-radiation detection is up and running, signal already incoming. Sending to speakers."

A series of short and long tones played over speakers in the room. Most were unable to interpret them, but one of the new arrivals, Ambassador Anderson, tilted her head to the side. "Next... interval... envoys... this one is the same, it— wait." She started jotting letters on a paper. "Prepare... here... okay, this one says, 'Envoys here, prepare for arrival next interval.'"

"That's got a lot of overlap with, 'Envoys come please wait check in next interval,'" said Ji-min.

"They're clearly working from a limited vocabulary," said Anderson. "Please send: 'Ready to receive envoys next interval.' But say 'beat' at the end instead of interval, they're using a different word for it."

"Sending," Ji-min said. They typed the message into

their console. Ames Mallway's software turned it into a simple digital signal, fed to the active portion of one of their decommissioned subspace drives, feeding it enough power to emit mu-radiation in pulses forming the message in Spacer's Morse, but not with enough power so as to break into p-space on its own.

Everyone waited. The signal from the other side stopped, and did not resume before the rift closed again. Silence hung in the room.

"Well. That's that." Ambassador Anderson nodded to Iyapo, then left the room.

"Thank you, Dr. Morgan," said Siobhan, "your team's work has opened a diplomatic channel that will soon see representatives from two different universes conversing for the betterment of all."

"You flatter me, Ambassador," said Iyapo wryly. "Folks, get them what they need for now, then hopefully they can keep the talks going somewhere else without us holding their hand. If you're looking for thanks, wait for the history textbooks. Nobody will care who talks to the Destroyers, people will care about who made it possible."

Eliyas doubted that. The only reason he hadn't complained first was that he generally couldn't stand whiners. He didn't care what history might think of him, but being treated as mere technicians by the head of the newly arrived ambassadorial team ground his gears.

Still. Iyapo had the right of it. Get them what they needed and they wouldn't be a problem for much longer.

A few people rotated out; the next interval was going to be an important one. Eliyas was intent on staying at his station, maybe marking up some of the raw data from the transmissions, and reluctantly taking a break for the washroom when the need arose.

Naturally, that was when Siobhan caught him in the hall.

"What do you think the envoys will be like?" she asked as he left the lavatory.

"Don't care." He considered, for a brief moment, ducking back into the room for solitude, before soldiering on.

"Will they look like us? A species we know? Or from a totally different galaxy altogether?"

"Don't care."

"I wonder if humans even exist in p-space. If everything is exactly the same except for that."

"There is absolutely no way that in a universe with even slightly different physics, that the evolution of-" Noticing the smug look on Siobhan's face, Eliyas cut himself off and huffed. "Listen, just assume that to whatever reasonable speculations you have my answer is, 'Don't care,' and to whatever fantastical suppositions you make, you get to make up some marvelous tirade on my part telling you that you're wrong, and keep it *all in your head* so I don't have to be party to it."

They continued back to the control room, Siobhan unconcerned with Eliyas' reproach. As they finally reached the door, she made a noise then said, "I wonder where they'll stay during negotiations."

"Siobhan!"

She just looked at him with a smile on her face; after a moment, Eliyas found that the rest of the room was also looking at him, not smiling. Well, forget them. He huffed back to his station and donned a headset, wishing fervently it were noise-canceling.

In the periphery of his awareness, Iyapo intercepted Siobhan, and they spoke in low voices. He caught snatches of the conversation; between "provoke", "response", "danger" and "professional", he wasn't sure whether the topic being discussed was himself or the Destroyers. "Bull-headed", however, made it quite plain.

"I am... *right* here."

Iyapo turned to him. "If you act like a child, we'll treat you like one and talk as though you're not in the room."

"Easy, Dr. Morgan." Siobhan put her hand on his arm, then addressed the room. "This is an important moment. Not the one we thought we were working toward, but still important, and a moment that requires our focus. Not childish games and quips. To that end..." She took a breath and stepped forward. "Sorry, Eliyas. I let that get away from me, and I shouldn't have. There will be time enough to be a thorn in your side *after* history is made."

Eliyas hmphed. He'd have rather been left alone, but of course now he had to say something. "Apology accepted, Dr. Doyle. I..." He paused, and deflated. "I should not have snapped at you in such a manner. To answer your earlier question: I do not much care what the envoys will look like. I simply hope they come with true intentions, and if they do not, then that is what the newly reinforced armada of Terran Orbital Defense, Jendeeri Police Fleet and other allied vessels are here for. Concern for who they are and what they do is not our job; our job is to ensure safe transit to p-space if required and otherwise to be ready for anything else. And to that end..." He stood from his console and walked up to the two of them. "Iyapo, if you will excuse me, I am going to go lie down for an hour and a half. Please retrieve me an hour prior to the next interval if I am not here by then."

"I... yes, that seems like a good idea, Eliyas. And I also, uh, ap—"

"Accepted. Just... stop making it so weird." Eliyas shook his head and left the room.

* * *

When he came back, just shy of two hours later, he had to admit that the nap had done him some good. He nodded to Iyapo, Siobhan, and a few others as he entered, and wordlessly took his seat again.

The control room filled up over the next hour. Anderson was again back in the room, this time flanked by a jendeer and a shiwiik. Nobody quite knew what the Destroyer envoy planned, so they were ready to communicate from the control room, and likewise there was a shuttle on standby if they decided to head out to meet the Destroyer ship.

In what seemed like no time at all, the interval was upon them.

"Rift is open and stable," reported Siobhan.

"Please send message: 'Ready to receive envoys.'"

"Message sent, Ambassador."

"Incoming message. Dr. Kim, please cease broadcast, the equipment can't differentiate signal sources."

"Of course, Dr. Omarov. Will cease after its second repetition. Should be... now."

"That sounds cleaner. Ambassador?"

"Sending... envoys... prepare... for... I'm not sure what that last word is. They're coming."

At that moment, a second rift opened up beside the first. While the initial experimental rifts at Alpha Point had been prismatic portals that distorted at least three dimensions of space and time, further calibrations of the equipment had stabilized the rifts to the point where they were almost the monochrome bright light exhibited by normal subspace travel, with only flashes and ripples of color and other emissions at the edges. This incoming second rift looked perfectly normal, erupting in bright light about half a kilometer away from the first.

Ambassador Anderson leaned forward, clearly ready for

the moment that would make her career. Eliyas didn't care about the moment with nearly the same personal investment, but he was still curious what would come out of that portal (not that he would admit such to Siobhan). One of the terrifying Destroyer warships? Something built along similar lines, but different somehow, less fear-inducing than a military vessel? Eliyas supposed it wouldn't even be recognizable at all. An entirely alien civilization, coming in peace and (hopefully) not in war—who even knew what their ships for that purpose might look like? After all, a jendeer and a human ship for the same purpose shared only the barest similarities of form in their design, and even a human freighter shared only the barest geometric similarities to a human warship with which it shared almost no function.

Mostly, though, the small, irrational part of him that he had trouble admitting existed was worried about receiving a flood of warships, one more invasion which would not be stopped at Alpha Point, which would not stop at Earth, which would continue to roll through the galaxy to finish what they had started, all those millennia ago.

Everyone had their own speculation, their hopes and worries, their own expectations of what they might see come through that portal.

What nobody expected to emerge from the rift was an erupting fireball.

Chapter XVI

The Admiral of the 106th Expedition Outside waited pensively as the Destroyer captives taken by the 107th returned back Outside, carrying with them that fleet's Historian.

Taut Syndicate of Unclaimed Stars was not as trusting as the Admiral of the 107th. Had the captives been hers, they would have been kept on the flagship or even brought to a planet where they could do no damage. They were Destroyers, and not just any Destroyers but Destroyers of the Beat. They were crafty and—to bring it back around—they were not to be trusted.

But Coarse Masonry of a Shattered Well was, in Taut Syndicate's opinion, a fool. That is why he had been sent to the other unchained Cries, smaller and more infrequent than those by which Taut Syndicate had been stationed, and it was only through serendipity that his smaller fleet had made contact before hers.

The Destroyers' ship closed with the portal Outside, and transited. The incoming portal—a rough, painful thing—

closed, and after a few moments, the outgoing portal closed as well.

There was nothing to do but wait.

It would have been good to have kept an open line Outside, so that reports could flow freely. But maintaining a portal took exponentially more energy the longer it was kept open. They simply had to wait for another portal to open, the Historian updating the fleet on how the talks progressed.

It was a lot to ask of Taut Syndicate, to be patient while the fate of a Historian was on the line. Not that the Admiral, esteemed as she was, cared much for Historians themselves; but what this Historian represented, in this instance, was the charge and aegis of being a diplomatic envoy. Taut Syndicate had no faith in the Destroyers to be civilized enough to respect diplomacy, regardless what their messages through the portals had said. They had not used diplomacy centuries ago when the 87th Expedition Outside had initially been stranded Outside, instead gathering and observing their misfortune. They had not attempted diplomacy during the much more recent Expedition, either; though their off-Beat Cries had ended, the Expedition had not returned, and Taut Syndicate felt that even if the Destroyers had met the Expedition at a bargaining table, they were cruel and vicious and underhanded enough to annihilate them anyway and keep them from returning.

These views are public record; in fact it is testimony to such ends that had seen Taut Syndicate awarded the Admiralty of the 106th.

It was expected that the gathered fleets would have to wait until the next Beat to hear any news back, as this location had never Cried out of time with the Beat. But this, too, proved the devilry of the Destroyers; when not even a quarter of the usual time between Beats had passed, a portal again opened, an unchained Cry in space.

"We are receiving a report," said the communications officer on duty.

"Decode and translate," said Taut Syndicate. By her appearance it seemed that a stone had uncomfortably settled in her thorax.

It took time to translate flashes of Breath to alien letters, and assemble them into unfamiliar words, and to translate those words to something civilized. When the officer had done so, they trembled. "'Envoys suffered malfunction coming out of ...' unknown word, possibly 'portal'. 'Ship destroyed, can not recover debris or people.'" The officer looked up at the Admiral and shrank back on their hind leg.

The Admiral stood still, then inhaled once, slowly. "So be it. Their treachery knows no bounds, and a Historian is dead. Their cover story fools no one." Taut Syndicate allowed no argument to their conclusion. "They do not deserve our response; only our retribution." The bridge crew steeled themselves. Some had been ready for this moment since arriving on-station. Some would later confide that they believed that the only reason Taut Syndicate had agreed to the plan to send the Historian back on the Destroyer vessel was the knowledge that the Destroyers could not be trusted with diplomacy, and Taut Syndicate had foreseen this occasion, and welcomed this definitive justification for the Expedition to set forth.

"Transmit to the entire 107th Expedition Outside: We will venture Outside before the next Beat drums and seek our resolution. We will punish those who took advantage of the flag of diplomacy and slaughtered our Historian. Then we will proceed to every place that Cries and silence them. We will not tolerate the Beat. To do so demeans us. We are the Protectors! We have failed to protect the Historian, and we have failed every single person in this galaxy that has had to live under the Beat for so long. No more—on this day, at long last, we will *stop* these Destroyers from terrorizing our homes!"

A cheer went up among the bridge crew as they set to work. The communications officer again spoke up. "Admiral, transmission link request from Admiral Coarse Masonry."

Taut Syndicate growled. "He will likely attempt to sway us from our path. Very well. Connect him, but observe the weakness that has plagued us for too long."

With a click of connection, a fuzzy hologram of the Admiral of the 107th stood on Taut Syndicate's bridge. "Taut Syndicate, stand your fleet down. We must report these circumstances home and seek counsel before we draw this galaxy into a war."

"Coarse Masonry," Taut Syndicate replied with restraint, "we will do no such thing. The 106th is tasked with the protection of all, and this act is a clear declaration of war. We know that the Destroyers have discovered how to come Inside; if we do not act now, we will be on the back foot as they invade."

"And if this was an accident as they state, then our preemptive strike will spur them to action where they had intended none before. They have advanced since the days of the 87th; your predecessor never returned and their objective was only two locations."

"And that is why our Expeditions today are outfitted not for recon but for *war*. *That* is our charge, and you cannot be so squeamish as to shy away from it, *Admiral* Coarse Masonry of a Shattered Well."

"Admiral, every time we have fought the Destroyers, *any* Destroyers, it has been when they are first exploring the fabric between Inside and Outside. We do not know the military prowess of these Destroyers, now that they have had so long to continue existing."

"Another reason that we should never have allowed them to continue existing in the first place!" Taut Syndicate was more impassioned than ever. "This is a wrong that must be righted, and now that their intentions are clear, we must act to counter them."

"Our mandate is not to enact war on the Destroyers," said Coarse Masonry. "It is to ensure that these unchained Cries do not present an imminent threat."

"They can come here, Coarse Masonry! You saw this yourself, face to face with these Destroyers, and yet you delude yourself on the threat this constitutes."

"We must reestablish communications," he pressed on, "and know everything we must before we jump to such a conclusion."

"What we *must* do is retaliate against the Destroyers. They told us what happened; they taunt us with the death of our Historian! They know what they are doing. Any time spent attempting to communicate with these savages is time that you are not getting ready to crush them for their misdeeds."

"You are making a grave mistake," said Coarse Masonry quietly. "You misinterpret your mandate and you may misinterpret what they have sent, all to your own ends."

"You may interpret your mandate and this treachery however you like," said Taut Syndicate by way of dismissal, "but the Protectors of the 106th Expedition Outside will not stand by. We will do what we must. You will either join us or stand aside."

The Admiral of the 107th glared wordlessly, then cut their end of the connection. Taut Syndicate took a moment to compose herself, and glanced around the bridge. If she was embarrassed at raising her voice to her supposed peer, she did not show it; but she drank in the pride she saw around her, pride in *her* and what *she* would do, and she knew that she had done, and was going to do, the right thing.

She was going to lead the Protectors to war.

ACT THREE

Chapter 17

The *Wadja* floated in space, unnoticed.

After its calamitous arrival through the portal, it had drifted through the cordoned-off area used for subspace rift testing, and then precipitously close to the small yet growing armada of military vessels protecting Alpha Point, then the installation itself. Now, it slowly tumbled towards the void at the jump point, where ships hung in space after arriving from, or making ready to depart to, to the rest of civilization.

A voice spoke up in the dimmed bridge of the ghost ship. "Fry. Have I told you how happy I am that the stealth tech is holding?"

"'Bout four times now, Cap'n. Still holdin', uh, indefinitely. 'Til it doesn't."

"Marvelous, let me know if it goes."

"Sure thing, Cap'n, you'll want to know to be properly embarrassed when everyone sees us with our pants down."

"Bold of you to assume I have dignity, Frystekh."

"Captain. How far do you plan on going with this?"

Hock turned his attention away from the conversation with his engineer, peering at his human crew member. "As far as it takes to get us to some quiet backwater system to go back to life as normal. Well, not too quiet, we need to make a tidy little profit, after all."

"Oh, sure, that's fine," said Liz, lounging at her station, spinning her hat around her finger. "That's what we're all here for and absolutely looking forward to doing." She snapped her hand closed around the brim, arresting the tricorn's movement. "I was wondering how far you're going to take our *guests*. Language barrier or no, our story won't hold water for... well frankly, the fact that they haven't forced the issue yet surprises the hell out of me."

"I agree," said Threm, somewhat to Hock's surprise. "I didn't sign up for no kidnappin'. Save our pelts, yeah, but we gotta do somethin' sooner or later with 'em."

"We can't keep sayin, 'We'll figure it out soon,' Cap," added Liz. "Soon is now and we need to at least have a solid plan."

Hock sighed theatrically, then spun his fins. "Well then what do you suggest? Box them up with a time delay beacon and a sticky note saying, 'Destroyer envoys enclosed'?" He stopped and thought for a moment. "Actually I rather like that idea."

"Ugh, I do too, and I hate that." Liz shook her head. "Okay. We need: First, to drop off the Three Musketeers back there. Second, to resupply; we're dangerously low on food and we torched most of our fuel reserves in that little combustible decoy. Third, to find out how to use our jump drive because no matter how good this stealth system is, they will *notice* if we try to hitchhike on a Jump Ferry."

"Hey-hey, I would argue with the order of operations there."

"Then find something that lets us do all three at once," Liz snapped. "Because doing any of the three will tell 'em we're here, and we gotta leave as soon as we're noticed. Or did you not see the fleet out there?"

"I happened. To see it," Hock replied icily. "Yes, Liz. Thank you. And I've been—"

A commotion rang out through the ship. Liz's board pinged. "Go ahead," she said, keying it.

"Uh, they got out, the bug one wants t' talk to the cap." Dekk was keeping his composure pretty well, considering the Destroyer's desire was more likely expressed as a demand than a request. And said Destroyer outsized him by a factor of four.

"Sure, Dekk, thank you," said Hock, taking over from Liz. "Tell him I'll be down shortly, we're in the middle of, ah, making sure—"

"That not needed," said Blade. There was rustling on the other side of the connection. "I move through your ship fine. You saw. I come to you."

Hock had indeed seen how well Blade could move, when he'd led him to the cargo bay when the Destroyers had arrived on the *Wadja*. Though his torso was almost as wide across as the passageways, the huge arthropod had navigated his way through the pirate vessel with ease. The way he'd spun and pushed off all of the available surfaces spoke to either his species spending evolutionary time in microgravity or Blade just being very proficient at it. Hock had guessed the first, because that sounded more fun; but now that the massive inhabitant of another universe was potentially upset and clearly able to free himself from the cargo hold and navigate the *Wadja* without impediment, Hock wondered why he'd ever attributed "fun" to him in the first place.

"Yes, ah, Dekk, if you would please be so kind as to lead Blade here, we would be happy to, ah, apprise him of the situation and current plan. Which we absolutely have ready to go at a moment's notice and would be *honored* to receive him as part of the festivities."

"Of course, Cap. Uh, I'll bring him to you through Blue deck?"

Bless his heart, Dekk was buying them a whole twenty extra seconds to scheme. "That would be just *perfect*, Dekk, thank you. We will see you shortly, Blade." Hock motioned for Liz to cut off the board. "Okay, I'll admit it, I didn't really have a *plan* ready, I had an *idea* that involved hijacking a ship and taking their navigation package and leaving Blade & Co. behind, but correct me if I'm wrong but isn't the only ship in the system that would have anything like nav data the *Jendeer military Jump Ferry?!*"

"You... might be wrong, Cap'n," said Ssswoorssepp. "I don't recognize where we are at all, constellation mapping doesn't return any known system in our nav. So—okay, no, straight to the point." She took a deep breath and said quickly, "We know that before the Battle of Earth humans were experimenting with subspace tech and it doesn't make sense that they were doing it near Earth where everyone could see it so they probably had a deep space black site for their illegal science experiments and we already know that the material from the battle was being shipped somewhere else so if I were them and wanted to keep doing research on it it'd probably be right back here and those new experiments are probably why the Destroyers noticed them here again and why these diplomatic negotiations are happening here."

And that's when the door to the bridge opened, with Dekk leading the massive form of Blade through the door. Half of the crew on the bridge stared at them, and the other half at Ssswoo.

"Ssswoorssepp. Be a dear and continue that train of

thought," said Hock carefully, studiously trying not to acknowledge the newcomers.

"I... just think that we will have more options for where to find working subspace drives, and navigational software." She swallowed nervously. "I am reviewing my logs now and will try to find a ship that made for the station from the jump point but maybe not from the Jump Ferry."

"Maybe." Hock inhaled, exhaled, put on a smile, and then turned to Blade. "My dear ambassador, welcome to the bridge of the good ship *Wadja*. As you may have overheard, we are currently putting the... *finishing* touches on our plan. Now, I am ashamed to admit that we are not the upstanding paragons of civilized law-abiders that we may have intimated that we are, but—"

"You are pirates."

Hock stopped mid-theatrics and blinked. He realized, first, that he was speaking a bit too floridly for the Destroyer to have comprehended everything (not that he cared), and second, that Blade would have had to *learn* the word "pirate" and wondered sorely who in his crew had told them such a thing. It was probably Carlos. He then realized, third, that everyone was looking at him while he hung there with his mouth agape. He closed it and smiled again. "Yes, Blade, we are dangerous ne'er-do-wells and ruthless buccaneers, scourge of commerce and... well, so on and so forth."

"You are pirates," Blade repeated. Hock still didn't have a read on facial expressions for his species; everything just came out as "nonplussed". Maybe such nonverbal emotional cues were in Blade's posture; but since that hadn't changed since he had entered the room, Hock was forced to assume that "nonplussed" applied to that, too.

"Yes. Well, you can see how that might present an issue for normal diplomatic channels. So upon entering the, ah, operational area, we engaged our proprietary stealth systems and have been sitting unnoticed, waiting for our chance."

"I wish to see the area." Blade carefully stepped towards Hock's spot at the center of the bridge. Hock backed away a touch and nodded to Ssswoo; she quickly put a general plot of the area on the main screen, then went back to her work. Blade pivoted his body a few ways to get a good look, and pointed one oversized claw at the indicators all over the display. "What are those?"

"Well. This one is us. This here is the science installation that made it possible for this diplomatic meeting to exist... these are some civilian freighters supplying the base. And all of these..." Hock swam out to the screen and situated himself in front of a mass of nearly a hundred contacts in various groupings. "These are military vessels."

"That is... much."

"Yes, a bit excessive, but then you did nearly destroy our civilization a few millennia ago so who can blame them. *Anyway.*" Hock tried to turn the conversation before Blade could object. "Because this facility—"

"We defended ourselves." *Drat. That didn't work.* "Your Cries hurt us. We had to stop you."

"Yes, and you *did* so with some light *genocide*, very good, can we just—"

"We destroyed your science and leadership. We left *you* alive." Blade gingerly turned to Hock, taking care not to hit anybody with his rear leg. Liz swayed away as she almost got stepped on. Threm, meanwhile, was paralyzed in shock at Hock trying to Captain Corven his way through a conversation with a Destroyer. "This is what we do," Blade continued. "You stay alive. But not a threat. This is how it always is. You made the Beat and it was an acceptable compromise."

"Listen, I don't want to argue with—"

"Not argue. Tell. I am the Teller. This is our history and the history of all encounters with your kind. This is the history laid forth by the College of History and Recalled by Porous Kin, Waking from Ignorance, which I now Tell to you. I cannot Tell what will happen now, or in the future. That is not my place."

"*Fine*," said Hock, "thank you for the history lesson, Professor. Now, maybe we can get back to our genius plan that lets you meet with the diplomats on that station and keeps everyone happy and not genocidey?"

Hock imagined that Blade looked like he wanted to continue arguing the point, but then conceded that he had fulfilled his obligation to Tell, or whatever. He nodded to Hock. "Proceed."

Hock glanced at Ssswoo, who was still working. "Weee are going to rendezvous with... *a ship*... and get things that we need, namely more supplies and a software package for our jump drive system. Because we value peace between the realms, or whatever, trust me we do. But we also value our way of life and our livelihood. So we get what we need to keep doing our thing without any of the relevant authorities poking their snouts in, and we drop you off with the honest, legitimate crew who would be more than happy to deliver you to whatever summit awaits you."

Blade's face swiveled under the exoskeletal carapace, taking in the bridge and, probably, working on translating some of what Hock had said. Finally, he said, "Acceptable." He carefully turned back to the screen full of dots and paths. "And which one will be unwilling part of your plan?"

"This one," said Ssswoorssepp at *exactly* the right moment, bless her, bless this whole crew. An isolated arrowhead lit up, near the station—and not too far from where the *Wadja* drifted. "The *PWK Swiftpack*. Earth-registered, non-military ownership, and most importantly its vector over time suggests that it came from the jump point but not the Ferry itself. It's been sitting in a waiting pattern for the last hour, but I'm guessing the station has more important things to worry about."

"Like that?" said Tenta. Hock checked the screen, then focused his eyes through it to the viewport behind, where multiple subspace rifts were opening up.

"Hey-hey, perfect timing! A distraction. Dekk, would you please escort our good Blade back down to the cargo bay with his companions?" He bobbed towards the screen, indicating the *Swiftpack's* icon. "Their connecting flight is here."

Chapter Eighteen

The Destroyer ships poured through subspace rifts, unmistakably martial, the same deadly harbingers out of jendeer mythology that had been made real in orbit of Earth not even a year ago. Eliyas thought, in a detached sort of way, about how nobody ever talked about Destroyer Jump Ferries; but then, as the reason for a Ferry was to consolidate the mu-rad signature to avoid reprisal from the Destroyers, the Destroyers themselves would naturally have no need of them.

The alien warships hung in space; if past experience was any indication, they'd be fully online in a couple of minutes.

"Get that pulse beacon online!" said Ambassador Anderson; a few hours ago, she had been utterly presentable, ready to receive the Destroyer envoys. She was mildly less so now, and jumped at a chance to salvage the situation.

"Mu-rad emitter online. Message?" replied Ji-min professionally, only the barest hint of panic in their voice.

"Play it as though they are not here to retaliate, we don't know their intentions for sure. Message: "Welcome. We offer condolences for loss of original envoy team. Ready to receive new envoys."

"Got it." They typed it in, checked it, and sent it to the transmission device. "Transmitting. Accelerated the send speed, message sends in twenty seconds, waits twenty seconds for a return, transmits again."

Anderson nodded in response and mumbled a "thank you". Eliyas kept half of his attention on the room and the rest on the scopes; sure enough, his readout was drowned out by the transmitted signal half the time, but after it cleared he made sure to focus. "Keep receiving telemetry," he said quietly to the observation team. "We have the most advanced sensors in the galaxy pointed at them. We want to see their startup sequence, we want to see how they communicate to each other, and if it's mu-rad we want to look for signs of modulation. If it comes to it, we want to see what emissions they give off while fighting." The others nodded in response.

Eliyas idly remembered, months ago, talking to some jendeer historian in his office, and he remembered that when they had first arrived, the Destroyers had been bleeding much more mu-radiation than normal. Sure enough, when they weren't getting overwhelmed by the communication signal, his scopes were showing mu-rad levels far exceeding those that remained after a normal subspace rift closed. A regular ship normally emitted mu-rad after a jump like a bar of steel coming out of a particularly warm room emitted heat; the Destroyer ships, by comparison, were smoldering like the remains of a campfire.

Iyapo approached Eliyas. "May I have a moment of your time?" he asked in a low voice.

Eliyas glanced at Iyapo, who was visibly nervous, and figured he wanted to speak with him elsewhere. But these readings were, potentially, too important. "I'm listening."

If Iyapo was thrown off by Eliyas refusing to leave his station, he didn't show it. "If this becomes a shooting situation... I won't know what to do. You?"

"If the shooting starts, that's why they're all here." He nodded out the viewport, indicating the massed fleet near the Destroyers. They were at least double the Destroyers' number, but the Destroyers had in the past easily bested fleets of the galactic community; the only reason they'd been defeated in Earth's orbit was the Jendeer Police Fleet getting the drop on them and flanking them. "If they start losing, then we can consider evacuation. Until then, these are valuable readings."

"Can you... take charge here? If that happens?"

Eliyas furrowed his brow at his screen. He considered ignoring Iyapo for what... had he seen something? But no. He kept his eyes on his screen but said, "Dr. Morgan. Iyapo. You are doing well. You are a person they will all follow, and they trust you'll have their best interests at heart." He spared him a glance. "They won't give me the same trust. If you say to evacuate, I won't argue with you. This is your operation now. Has been for some time."

Iyapo was stunned, which had the fortunate benefit of letting Eliyas focus on his work again. "El- Eliyas, thank—"

"Sh." He grabbed a headset and played with a few dials. "I'm taking one of the mu-rad dishes. I'm—damn it." He pulled the earcup away as Ji-min's mu-rad Morse code blasted the instruments again.

"What did you see?" said Iyapo.

"Not sure. Possible mu-rad signature close to the base." He counted down the rest of the twenty seconds then slipped the headset back on. Iyapo crowded behind him, the question of leadership now long gone.

"Destroyer ships powering up. Viewport lights. No unexpected emissions. Nothing in mu-rad yet—wait, getting broadcasts now." Siobhan had been paying attention from across the room, and apparently had cloned Eliyas' workspace to keep an eye on the Destroyer vessels. "Can't decode, obviously, looks like noise to our sensors. Running Dr. Mallway's package on it... definitely a different profile than we give off!"

"Fascinating, are they responding to our beacon?"

Both she and Eliyas growled and took their headsets off again. "I'll tell you in twenty seconds," said Siobhan.

"Sorry," Ji-min replied.

"Don't be, they have a window to respond in and they should realize it in another loop or two." They set back to their tasks when the response window opened up again.

"Getting some stray ionizing radiation," said someone to Eliyas' right. "Could be weapons powering up."

"Get a message off to the fleet," said Anderson to her shiwiik teammate. "They are *not* to fire first." The avian squawked in acknowledgment.

"Bingo," said Eliyas, "I've got a mu-rad signature coming from empty space near one of our supply freighters." Ji-min's message sent again and Eliyas looked at Iyapo. "Looks like *someone* got through."

Iyapo looked uneasy, and called to Anderson. "Ambassador, we have a potential Destroyer contact broadcasting mu-rad on approach to one of our supply freighters. No ship on scopes, maybe they're in spacesuits?"

"Is it a strike team?" she mused. "Why the freighter, why not us, why are they broadcasting?" She turned to her companions. "I need ideas!"

While the ambassadors conferred, Siobhan said, "Remember when we saw another mu-rad spike during testing? Do you think that whatever ship was causing that might have leaked... other tech to them?"

Everyone shook their heads; they'd passed off the

readings and made it someone else's problem. Eliyas didn't want to consider what it might mean for the Destroyers to have stealth technology. "Should we be communicating with them?" said Ames.

"We're broadcasting omni-directionally, whoever wants to respond will," said Anderson, rejoining the conversation. "We can't afford to prioritize that over the fleet while their intentions are unknown."

On cue, never having made a response to the hail, the Destroyer fleet opened fire, and two smaller friendly ships blew up immediately.

"And how about now," asked Iyapo, blood draining from his face.

The shiwiik ambassador squawked, while the other two let out more traditional curses. "I need this data collection," Eliyas told Iyapo, "can Ji-min keep transmissions to once a minute?" He was fully absorbed in his screens, and as Iyapo called out to Ji-min, Eliyas called sidelong to the others in his row, "Scoop it all up, call anything of interest that you see in real-time, the rest we can go over later."

"Ambassador," said Iyapo, "it appears the Destroyer fleet isn't interested in speaking. If you want to give it a shot, I think that freighter is your best bet."

Anderson looked at Iyapo, then back at one of the screens. "Very well, Dr. Morgan, you could be right. Krawwkteraak, let the shuttle pilot know we have a new destination, then stay here in case whoever's in charge of that death fleet out there changes their minds. Someone contact that freighter, let them know to expect the original diplomatic team. Zeffmerap, with me." The jendeer followed Anderson as they hustled from the room while the shiwiik called down to the hangar bay.

"Freighter *PWK Swiftpack*, come in, come in *Swiftpack*," called Siobhan.

Iyapo leaned down to Eliyas' terminal. "How's mu-rad look?"

"The only emissions I'm getting are probably communications, broadcasts so low-level I need to boost the gain. If that's comms and we've been blasting them with the normal-level mu-rad we get when we open a rift, no wonder they're upset at us."

"That sounds an awful lot like speculation," said Iyapo wryly.

"I'll admonish myself when I have time." Eliyas winced as another allied vessel, this one a shiwiik cruiser, cracked in half, a loss only halfway tempered by a smaller Destroyer vessel meeting a similar fate. "Looks like that signature from near the freighter is stronger, maybe they're realizing that with the strength we're outputting, our receivers aren't as sensitive. And our sample rate just isn't up to the task, there's some variance in the strength of the signal but I just don't have the tools here to see the full waveform. Assuming mu-rad is a wave and not a particle. Or... oh god dammit, you jendeer morons, you couldn't have even figured that out for us."

Iyapo clapped him on the back with more unconcern than his face showed. "We'll get it in time. Siobhan, how's the freighter?"

She held up a finger. "Roger that, *Swiftpack*, keep us updated. We'll let you know when the shuttle is on its way to you." She signed off then said, "They know there's a phantom signature coming their way and will hold fast. Captain said she'd go along with anything as long as it doesn't come from the furball out there."

"Good." Iyapo took a breath to try to steady himself as the battle waged on outside. "Cooler heads will prevail. Let's just hope they get that chance."

Chapter XIX

The 106th Expedition Outside set upon the Destroyers with a righteous fury. Officers and enlisted alike knew that the time had come to strike back against those from Outside.

But things did not progress as they had been told.

When the 105th Expedition Outside had set out, not long ago, in this galaxy, to combat the Cries that spurned the Beat, they had been lost. They had been sent to explore, to determine the reason for the rhythmless Cries, and if possible, to correct it. They had not been outfitted for war. But their mission had succeeded.

The loss of the 105th was mourned, but also taken as an object lesson—should the need arise for another Expedition into this galaxy, they must be stronger. And so both the 106th and 107th Expeditions Outside had been furnished with the capacity for war, each with double the ships of their predecessor.

Admiral Taut Syndicate of Unclaimed Stars was grappling with the fact that it may not be enough.

There was no doubt that this fight would be won.

Another Destroyer ship succumbed to the Protectors' virtuous fire as she considered the situation. But the losses sustained would be far more than any Expedition had suffered in its first engagement.

But then, the Destroyers had been expecting them here. Perhaps it would be simpler once past this vanguard.

In the aftermath of the battle, with great attention paid to internal status monitoring systems, the following events had to be carefully reconstructed. They were not Observed at the time, so subtle was the coordination. Speculation is best left to others; what history knows, however, is this:

The Admiral's personal communicator pinged, and she ignored it as she directed ships into a faltering gap in the enemy's defenses. Even having such a device on her person was considered an unnecessary distraction in a battle situation.

The communications officer managed to make eye contact, and made an unknown gesture with their front claw, and the Admiral stole a glance at their communicator. Upon reading the message, the Admiral inputted a quick reply, then returned her full attention to the battle.

Elsewhere in the flagship, a personal communicator pinged that belonged to the gunner on the flagship's third gun. They read the message, and injected a quick program into their targeting system. According to the ship's computer diagnostics, this gunner was still firing on their assigned targets. Nobody looked close enough at the time to see that they were in fact not hitting Destroyer vessels. They were not even aiming at the targets, not even firing when diagnostics said they were.

According to environmental monitoring, the gunner loaded a different targeting profile into their station. They then proceeded to fire. According to any external observers, their gun started malfunctioning, firing in random directions, but a quarter of the shots were aimed at a specific spot in space. There was nothing there, the shots missing even the closest Destroyer vessel, a noncombat vessel near the installation, by a wide margin.

This all took time, however; minutes to communicate and to load software and to begin firing. In the meantime, Taut Syndicate had another problem to worry about.

The 107th Expedition Outside was arriving into the theater of the battle.

The Admiral snarled as she watched the newcomers arrive and exhale the Breath that had carried them Outside. "Tell them to join in or stay out of the way," she yelled. "Keep telling them and don't let up until they've powered on and acknowledged."

"Yes, ma'am."

She watched her detachment chip away at the gap in the enemy's lines, when suddenly those same vessels started melting away as the enemy ships to either side rushed to cut them off from the main group.

Taut Syndicate cursed. Protector ships were situated with most of their guns facing forward, powerful weapons that used the spine of the ship to build great destructive power. These Destroyer ships used less powerful guns, but they were more spread around the vessels, making it harder for them to be caught unawares—as the detachment's ships were now so caught.

All of this was made worse as the accursed Destroyers kept broadcasting their primitive signal, hoping in vain to lull Taut Syndicate into a false sense of security and succeeding only in periodically impeding the fleet's coordination by utterly overwhelming the reception of the Breath.

The Admiral watched on as the tide of battle turned before her eyes. She growled, then said, "Tactical, rank each vessel from most dangerous to least. Then all ships will fire on a single vessel."

"Won't that waste—"

"*All ships.* Firepower distribution theory goes out the window when they're stronger than we anticipated. I want those ships gone."

"Yes Admiral! All ships!" Her orders were relayed. They were good orders, and afterward it was considered to be something that would have been effective against the Destroyers, although in her zeal, they were orders that would reveal the first thread that would unravel her duplicity.

"Does that include me, Admiral?" An image of Coarse Masonry of a Shattered Well appeared on the bridge as the ships of the 107th powered up.

"Of course it includes you," roared Taut Syndicate.

"I am here to observe," said the other admiral. His ships were still powering up, but had yet to fire.

Taut Syndicate sneered in response. "You cannot Observe. Your Historian is dead. Or had you forgotten what happened to them?"

The conversation was put on hold as the Destroyers again sent out their Breath. Taut Syndicate used the opportunity to take in how the battle had progressed and gave orders to be sent out to the fleet when the disruption had passed.

"I remember that we were told there was an accident," said Coarse Masonry after the disruption had passed, having no trouble picking up the conversation. Taut Syndicate considered that he had probably done nothing the entire time, thinking that this foolish line of inquiry was the most important thing he could be doing. "I have not been apprised of further developments. What new intelligence have you gathered?"

"I have *gathered* that these duplicitous conquerors have

amassed a warfleet that was ready to attack the moment we emerged Outside—" A Protector ship blew up as if to punctuate the point, even as another Destroyer ship fell. "—and have used *simple deduction* to conclude that they killed the Historian, and are trying to kill us, now I am *ordering* you to keep that from happening!"

Coarse Masonry nodded wordlessly, then consulted with someone outside of the hologram's field of capture. Another Breath disruption hit and Taut Syndicate again refocused her attention on the battle, seeing it continue to slip in the Destroyers' favor.

On the gunnery deck, the gunner stopped their errant firing, entered a quick message into their communicator, and unloaded their illicit code, then resumed the focused firing they had been assigned. Taut Syndicate received a message, glanced at it furtively, then ignored it, seemingly satisfied.

"Before I join the battle," said Coarse Masonry again, "I would ask one question of the Admiral of the 106th Expedition Outside." He drew himself up in height. "All of your vessels are concentrating fire on a single enemy, a strategy for which I must applaud you. All of your vessels... except your own. At what, exactly, was your third gun firing?"

Chapter 20

Liz didn't like it.

Sure, it was a solid enough plan—covertly communicate with the freighter, board it, get what they needed and drop off the Destroyers, then be on their way—it was among the most well-planned operations Hock had had in recent memory. But the problem was that the plan was needed in the first place.

She was furious with almost every decision Hock had made for the last month. She wasn't overly fond of the first subspace jump away from Earth, though they were still alive and any other unpleasantness only made it a bad proposition in retrospect; the *Wadja* had evaded system security before and possibly could have done so again. But she didn't fault Hock too much for that one.

Everything else, though. Just playing along with their alien captors and overlords for a month, not doing anything. Hock went on and on about waiting for opportunity, but he was just as scared as the rest of them. Liz had tried sharing a few ideas with him but he'd always shot them down.

Then when he did get an idea, he'd been too distracted

with his own brilliance and hadn't been paying attention, so he didn't realize that the Destroyer trio would be along for the ride. So he just twiddled around, said "this is fine" and "hey-hey" a few times, and... there it is, kidnapping and precipitating what could lightly be termed a *diplomatic incident* rather than just saying to the invading warfleet, "Hey, your ambassador is right here, maybe everyone could chill out a bit?"

An hour ago, while the *Wadja* was still drifting but before the Destroyer fleet had entered stage-other-galaxy to put on a light show, she'd gotten up to go to the head. Most of the crew stayed out of her way because they could tell she was upset; Carlos got in the way instead and asked what was wrong, like some kind of counselor. While everybody had been in the "playing-along-with-captors-and-overlords" mode, he'd continually done that, and of course she'd never shared her misgivings about the Captain's actions—she wouldn't even do so to other bridge staff, though she was getting close to thinking about maybe doing so, which honestly felt one step away from mutiny, and *Would that be so bad?*, and *Oh, no*—he still encouraged her, said that she was a great leader for the crew, and so on. Either he was sweet and naive and trying to make her feel better, or after living with non-humans for so long she'd forgotten how to hide her daily facial expressions and he'd read her like an open book, encouraging her thoughts without explicitly saying so.

Probably the second one. He's too perfect to not be, what's the term, "emotionally intelligent" like that.

Still. Even if he did tell her what she wanted to hear, the idea that the newest member of the crew—someone who until a month ago had been part of a system security force and, for all she knew, still felt allegiance to it—was surreptitiously telling her that she could run the ship better than Hock, made her back down from those same thoughts, at least a little. Get things done first, worry about the org chart some other time, because there was no trope she hated worse than the ill-timed mutiny.

I mean, if he's gonna get us all killed anyway... nope, not finishing that thought.

So now, even though literally every single authority in the system was worried about the Destroyer armada, Tenta was still getting as close as possible to the *PWK Swiftpack* and dropping into formation like a second legitimate freighter had been there the whole time that everyone just overlooked. Hock apparently thought that showing off to the overgrown bug taking up so much of the bridge was a better use of time.

"Captain," she finally snapped, "I bet Mr. San Martín's seen academy grads who are less precise than this. Can we *get a move on*, please?"

"Yes, Liz, thank you," said Hock, unflappable as ever. "Tenta, wonderful. Fovak, get me a link." Fovak hit a few buttons and nodded. "To the *PWK Swiftpack*, this is Captain Hock Corven of the *Wadja*. Under the authority of, well, myself, I must regrettably inform you that we will be boarding you, taking possession of some of your cargo and software, and in trade we offer a way for your friends to get out of this whole mess. Fry, if you please?"

The *Wadja* reappeared, again visible to the light-viewing world as its weapons bristled in the direction of the adjacent freighter. Hock grinned, ready for the freighter's captain to respond with surprise, to be cowed before the great Captain Corven, or to be indignant in some way for him to shut down with far too many words.

A window appeared on the viewscreen, presenting a human woman with short blonde hair, seated in a small flight deck, wearing sensible coveralls and a slight smile.

"Ah, we were wondering when you'd show up. We've been expecting you."

"You *what?*" cried Hock, and it was all Liz could do not to burst out laughing as he once again was denied his play at being a swashbuckling pirate.

"You have the Destroyer ambassadors, yes?"

"Destroyer," mused Blade. "That is your term for us? Fascinating."

"You, hush. Ah—yes, Miss, uh—"

"*Captain* Lindström. Pleased to make your acquaintance, Captain Corven, though I will say that yours being a pirate vessel is not a detail we had anticipated."

"Captain... Lindström. Likewise, a pleasure."

"By all means, Captain, please do come over and make yourselves at home. And make sure to actually bring your guests, they are doubly expected. What do they drink? We'll make sure to have a bucket of wine ready. Or beer, whatever we can find. Jenkins probably has a few stashed flasks somewhere we could avail ourselves of."

"Hey!" said a voice from off-screen. "That's mine!"

This woman was *out-sassing Captain Hock Corven!* Liz loved her. "Better do as she says, Cap'n," she added. "Looks like she's all compliant-like and ready for company."

Hock just glared daggers at her, then said to Lindström, "Yes, we will be over shortly. Let us know where to connect and we'll get this done right quick. Oh, dear Captain, are you in possession of a navigational system for subspace drives that *everyone knows* our ships are too small for?"

"I may be. You are not?"

"Oh, it's a long tale of woe that nonetheless serendipitously led to our being in this very position before you, I shan't bore you with it, but I should very much like to avoid making any more trips to another universe in the next little while, so if you can make that software suite easy for my crew to grab I would be most appreciative."

"Why, Captain Corven, I don't know that I much like the idea of such a thing as untethered subspace jump technology being in the hands—my apologies, fins—of such a fearsome reprobate such as yourself." Oh, *God*, she was enjoying the repartee, and Hock was back on his equilibrium, this was awful, Liz hated this woman.

"Well, be that as it may, due to the aforementioned *pirate* status of this vessel, we will be taking it anyway, and your cooperation is more to keep my talented but rushed technical team from damaging anything in the process."

"Hm, you drive a hard bargain, Captain. Put it that way, how could I say no? Send what you require and we'll get this done nice and quickly." She reached up and cut the connection.

"Well." Hock floated for a moment, then clapped his fins together. "Never a dull day. Let's head over then, yeah?"

"And not a moment too soon," said Ssswoo. "Looks like the Destroyer fleets are firing on each other, too. Our distraction might solve itself a bit quicker than we'd like."

"Then we hurry," said Blade.

Moments later, Hock, Liz, and a half dozen selected boarding crew, including Dekk with a portable workstation to grab the nav data and Blade bringing up the rear, were hustling through the *Wadja's* cramped passageways. Liz was shoving an earpiece into place and making sure her weapons were all set—a matched pair of pistols fashioned after historical flintlocks and a more utilitarian spare on the tragic off-chance they got separated. (The last time she'd boarded a ship she'd been stuck on translation duty, so she wasn't going to miss out on their comfortable wooden handgrips this time around.)

"Tenta, how are we doing?" Hock asked as the group rounded the last corner to the cargo bay.

"We're alongside, their cargo bay access umbilical is extending now. I explained that it'd be more convenient for our guests to come through there because of their size, Captain Lindström seemed pleased to accommodate."

"Of course she did." He opened the hatch to the bay, where Star and Kin were huddled in conversation. They looked up—possibly surprised, Star especially had an expressive face. Was that guilt? "Blade, would you be a dear and apprise your compatriots of the plan? We make contact..." A clanging sound reverberated around the hold from an exterior access hatch. "...now."

The Destroyers talked amongst themselves, raising their voices, and Liz wished she knew what they were talking about. Maybe it had something to do with how some stray shots from the battle had come improbably close (when then Blade had said something into a communicator of his own in his own language, and then there were no more close calls). She really should have been paying more attention, but no—and Liz saw Carlos trying to catch her eye. The devil on her shoulder himself. He wasn't part of the boarding party and, truthfully, she didn't have time for whatever he needed... but she went to him anyway. "Make it quick."

"Didn't know if you needed help. Don't really know how many in there will be up against you."

No, this guy definitely knew what he was talking about. Sure, there might be security troops on the freighter, but nothing that the *Wadja's* crew couldn't handle. But if she were to pull one of those famously stupid ill-timed mutinies, then maybe not everyone would take her side. It would depend on just how stupid a decision Hock would make that would necessitate such an action on her part in the first place.

Liz narrowed her eyes at Carlos, then decided she could use a wild card. "You any good with a gun?"

"Dishonor on my family, only seventh in my class."

She rolled her eyes and pulled her spare pistol from her waistband, handing it to him. She turned back to the group and saw Hock glowering at her. "Trust me," she said, unsure if he should. He harrumphed, and floated over to the hatch as it opened, the thicker atmosphere of the *Wadja's* cargo bay rushing into the umbilical until it equalized. He harrumphed again, readied his anti-grav harness, and led the way into the freighter.

Everyone piled into the collapsible passageway and the hatch closed behind them; then, as Liz's ears popped from the pressure change, the *Swiftpack's* hatch opened.

She expected the other shoe to drop and to see a battalion's worth of rifles pointed at them, but it was just Lindström and, probably, the flask-possessing Jenkins. She was standing at ease with a smile on her face, while Jenkins was glowering and stiff as a board. Liz was more cautious about the one with the inviting expression. Despite Liz's expectations, they were not in fact in the main cargo hold of the ship, but a smaller vestibule of sorts, still plenty large enough for the Destroyers.

The woman addressed Hock first. "Captain. Ambassadors, I presume," she added, looking at the three in back whose utterly alien forms towered over the rest. "Welcome to the *Swiftpack*. We don't have an umbilical for our hold, but it's just through here, if you think you can get through."

"We manage," said Star from the back. "Honored to be received."

"Let's get our esteemed guests situated first, Captain," said Lindström, "then we will see to your other needs."

"We are in quite a rush," Hock said, "but as you say, the

Ambassadors take precedent. Liz, take everyone into the hold, get them situated, and get us what we need. Jenkins, is it? Can you show me and Dekk here the cockpit so we can get that navigation package from you?"

Lindström nodded, and Jenkins made his way forward, the two kikan in tow. Everyone else piled into the cargo hold, though Kin needed a bit of time to find the optimal angle to squeeze in—he wasn't quite as malleable as most other species Liz had met.

The freighter reminded Liz of a miniature version of the barge they'd stolen the subspace and stealth tech from, the kind of thing meant to haul as much as possible with as small a crew as the bean counters could get away with. She felt a moment of sympathy for the likely overworked duo operating it, but quickly got over it. The *Swiftpack* clearly had the payload capacity to help supply an army, but for now the central zone of the expansive hold played host to only a single oversized cargo container, while partitioned sections around the edges were filled with pallets and smaller containers. Lindström pointed at two of the bays. "Three and five have everything you asked for, if you're in a hurry. The research installation will miss them, of course, but I was instructed to make sure the Ambassadors were safe and sound first and foremost." She looked Liz up and down. "I don't believe that negotiating with pirates was quite what they had in mind, but your supply request is more than reasonable."

"The subspace nav package, less so, I presume."

"Quite."

The two women stood staring each other down for another moment, then Liz said, "Alright, boys, two to a pallet, get that loaded up. Not you, Zipzi." She didn't trust him to lift a box of cereal without breaking it. The others got to work and quickly slung antigrav pods onto the pallets and worked them through the hatch.

Liz's earpiece pinged. "Dekk is plugged in, getting what we need now."

"Copy, Cap'n, I got the boys pullin' our pallets back to the ship."

"Good." There was a moment of silence as the unreal tableau of a fully cooperative ship let the pirates continue their boarding operations. "You know," Hock added, more quietly, "this is a nice ship."

"Yes, Captain Corven, it is," said Liz suspiciously.

"You, uh... you think we might take it?"

"No, I don't–!" Liz stopped herself, hoping Lindström couldn't hear anything.

Unfortunately, it seemed that up on the flight deck, Jenkins had heard just fine.

There was a muffled shout, then, "No, nothing! Just admiring your vessel, my good man, hey-hey!"

There was a sound of a scuffle on the other side, and Lindström must have seen Liz's face. She dashed to a panel by the hatch back to the vestibule and said, "Jenkins, report!"

The hatch next to her slammed shut, just as the second pallet of cargo passed through. Now the only ones left in the hold were Lindström, Liz, Carlos, Zipzi (damn), and the Destroyers. Carlos shoved his hand in the pocket he'd stuffed the pistol in, but Liz caught his eye and shook her head. Then, because Zipzi didn't do subtlety and his damn giraffe neck was swiveling all over, his own rifle pointed any way except where he was looking, Liz commanded, "Stand down!"

"Jenkins!" yelled Lindström.

There was banging on the hatch, and a muffled question

through it that came in more clearly on her earpiece. "Liz? What happened?"

"No idea," she told her crew. "Get the cargo onboard before Lindström's copilot does something stupid."

"Yes'm."

"He better not have. *Jenkins!*" the freighter's captain yelled again.

The scuffle in Liz's earpiece peaked, then stopped, and Hock's transmission cut off.

"Captain? Captain?!"

Jenkins replied first. "Everything is fine, Captain Lindström. You're all secure in the hold, yes?"

"Yes, Jenkins, we are, now what is going on up there and why did you close the hatch?"

"Cap'n? Liz? What's going on?" Fovak wanted an update, and Liz wished she had one.

"I'm multitasking, Åsa, don't worry about it."

"Bit of trouble. You should have the cargo incoming. Do not send anyone back over, I don't know how long we're gonna stay connected."

"What do you mean, multitasking? Anderson told us, we make sure the Ambassadors are here, everything else can wait! We were *ordered* not to multitask!"

"Copy that, Liz. Uh, getting a call from the hold, two pallets, four crew. That everyone?"

"Anderson has her priorities, I have mine. I'm afraid I haven't been entirely forward about my prior—and, as it turns out, present—employment, and if it weren't for a wanted criminal falling into my lap, we might've kept it that way."

"That's everyone I sent. Stand by."

"Jenkins, I reserve witty discussion for floating beach balls with swishy jackets, from *you* I want a *straight answer*— who are you and what are you doing?" Lindström leaned on the transmit button on the console like she could use it to press a proper answer from Jenkins.

There was a sigh on the other side of the channel and Liz leaned in close, exchanging worried looks with the freighter's captain. Finally, Jenkins replied, "I'm an agent of the Terran Intelligence Agency, reassigned to making sure that the supply lines to Alpha Point remain secure. My previous assignment was in Trappist. Where *this* man, *this* crew, and *this* ship are quite unfortunately well known." There was a pause, and the next transmission was also picked up by her earpiece and, presumably, any ships within range. "Crew of the pirate vessel *Wadja*, you are under arrest."

Chapter Twenty-One

"I wasn't *planning* on being intelligence overwatch during three concurrent operations," groused Eliyas as he swung another one of the sensor arrays towards the freighter. "Our readings are going to be absolute garbage."

"Pretend it's a stress test," said Iyapo, distracted. "We'll have our readings and if everything goes well we'll have some friends to help us with more controlled tests for new readings."

"If you can't make your own readings, store-bought is fine!" called Siobhan.

"What does that even mean?!"

"Yes, there," said Iyapo, ignoring them. "That's the *Swiftpack*, and that's definitely another ship docked with it. Do we have an ID?"

"Transmitting to the floor, if anyone knows what it is, say so."

"Doesn't look Destroyer." Everyone in the room glanced at the other screen, which was currently kept on the main event. The second wave of Destroyers had just started firing on the first, and between the two fleets there were plenty of examples of Destroyer starship construction. Most shared the black and red color scheme, the concept of a central core with protrusions of various shapes, and an occasional disregard for symmetry.

The ship docked with the *Swiftpack* didn't look like any of them. It was grungy, compact, and... old-looking, in a familiar way. Suresh looked close at it, clearly with some level of recognition. "Definitely seems like it's from our universe, kind of old, maybe a decomm—"

"Incoming!"

Heads again snapped their attention to the screen with the battle on it.

"No—I mean... sorry." Everyone looked slowly back towards Ji-min. "I meant, incoming transmission." They sheepishly flicked the incoming pulses to the room speakers.

Krawwkteraak, the shiwiik ambassador, cocked his head and listened to the repeating signal, then started mimicking it in a quick series of clicks as it started to loop. When the outgoing signal started to interfere, he kept clicking from memory, grabbed a pen and held it in his beak, and pulled it across a page, letting it oscillate as he repeated the pattern. Finally, he dropped the pen back to his wing-hand and set about translating. "One minute," he chirped.

"I'll, uh, end our broadcast in the meantime. Seems they got the message."

"You were saying," said Iyapo to Suresh, without taking his eyes off the ambassador.

He tilted his head back and forth, uncertainly. "The unknown has hallmarks of galactic patrol craft design from fifty to a hundred years ago, so it's probably a decommissioned security frigate. Not sure what species, or what particular security force, though. Looks, uh... this is going to sound stupid... looks rather like I might expect a pirate vessel to look."

Nobody immediately disagreed. "They have horrible timing," observed Siobhan. "Do you think that's our mu-rad source?"

"I don't know," said Eliyas, "the transmission cut out a little while ago. Could be unrelated but that's unlikely. For all we know they stole a drive and are the source of the mu-rad spikes we saw during testing. And they picked an astronomically bad time and place to ply their trade. And the supposed signal was just mu-rad bleed off since it's improperly calibrated." Eliyas was mumbling by this point, hoping nobody would notice his rampant speculation—or, at least, not comment on it. "Maybe we'll learn more when Ambassador Anderson's shuttle gets there. What are we looking at for their ETA?"

"*Awk*, ten minutes," said Krawwkteraak idly. Eliyas realized he'd barely heard the shiwiik speak before and he almost laughed at the incongruity of it even vocalizing the stereotypical parrot squawks as a verbal tic. "And I have this translated. 'We wish no harm. We apologize for Admiral *[long untranslatable]* actions. We not shoot you. You not shoot us.' Dr. Kim, if you would please transmit that we have received their message, three loops then wait a minute so your colleagues have a clear band." He slid to another console at his station. "Admiral Cooper, this is Ambassador Krawwkteraak. Come in."

"The admiral went down with the *Olympiad*, Ambassador, this is Captain Zhekhten of the *Hidden Tooth*."

"The new Destroyers are there to help you. The first fleet appears to be a rogue actor. Only fire on Destroyer vessels that are targeting you."

"Are you sure about that, Ambassador?"

"No, but either way they're already shooting each other.

I'd recommend not getting involved unless they force the issue."

"We've taken a beating out here and I don't mind not having to take them all on, if I believe you." There was a pause. "Which I'm not sure I do. But I don't mind a wait-and-see approach in case we actually have friendlies. Thank you, Ambassador, please update me with any further communications from the Destroyers."

"Thank you, Captain. *Awk*, if you've got a spare database officer, I'm sending you an image of an unknown vessel that has appeared in-theater, could use a basic profile ID."

"A bit busy but we'll throw it in the queue, thank—oh. Well, that won't be necessary. This is a kikan security schooner, commissioned about seventy years ago, patrolled supply lines during the Paikauhale Revolt. Was waylaid by a pirate, Captain Qenbke Rimtide, and was captured and given to his second, Hock Corven. Corven parted ways with Rimtide and continued the life of piracy, and he and his crew are wanted in two systems. The striping is new but I'd recognize those hull patch jobs anywhere."

Another transmission suddenly cut in. "Crew of the pirate vessel *Wadja*, you are under arrest." Everyone waited a moment, but there was no follow-up; clearly someone wanted to gloat publicly, but not conduct the nitty-gritty of business the same way.

"*Awk*, seems like you're not the only one who's brushed up on their patrol craft history."

"Indeed. Pretty poor timing."

"Seems to be a lot of that going around. Thank you, Captain."

"*Hidden Tooth*, out."

"Krawwkteraak to Anderson, come in."

Eliyas turned his attention away from the ambassador

filling in his colleagues, and tried to ignore the occasional squawk. "Next question is where they came from," he said. "We've got every instrument known to man strapped to this station, and a few we didn't even know about yet. We have to have picked up something aside from that mu-rad ghost signal."

"Any thoughts on why it was emitting mu-rad in the first place?"

"You know how I feel about speculation, Dr. Morgan," said Eliyas, frowning. "Especially when every explanation I think of is worse than the last. Let's get through this hour, then if we're not told the answer, then we can do some supposing."

"Fair enough. Siobhan, how's the battle looking out there?"

"Looks like it's dying down, in our favor. That fresh Destroyer fleet is still in good shape. Our fleets have taken a beating but with the relieved pressure have been able to regroup. The first Destroyer fleet is starting to feel the pinch."

"I've got mu-rad just spraying out of all of them. Clearly not doing any damage, has to be communications. Wish we could tell what they're saying."

"Say, Eliyas, odd question, but... their communications mu-rad. Transverse?"

"Ah—yes. Not getting anything longitudinal off of them at all."

"And our bursts?"

Eliyas held up three fingers, then two, one, then checked his scope as Ji-min's message sent out quickly. "Longitudinal. At the moment at least, unless we open a solo rift to p-space, if we generate mu-rad then it's one way, if they do then it's the other way."

"Fascinating. For some other time, obviously."

"No... this might actually be the perfect time." Eliyas stared at his screen for a moment, remembering something Siobhan had said, then asked, "Dr. Morgan, can you please take over mu-rad monitoring?" He stood and offered his chair to Iyapo.

"And what will you do?" he asked, sitting and draping the headset around his neck. "Are you..."

"No, you've still got this operation. I'm just going to pull up our instrument logs, see if I can figure out where our pirate friend came from." He took a seat at the empty console next to Siobhan and started making virtual copies of the logs, organizing them and working his way through. Starting in the present moment, he checked various instruments going back in time. With most of the instruments pointed toward the transit cordon-*cum*-battle zone, there hadn't been nearly as high a quality of data before Eliyas had turned one of the arrays. He started with a simple camera and scrubbed backwards, seeing the pirate vessel before it made contact with the *Swiftpack's* umbilical, and then... it disappeared.

That wasn't right. He went back forward, frame by frame. The camera wasn't a great one and only took a few shots a second, so in one frame, there was nothing; then over the course of two frames, it appeared, first in splotches against the starfield in the second frame, then fully there in the third.

He tapped his finger against his mouth, then took stock of where the ship was visible and attempted to trace the route backwards. It wasn't exact, but still showed a course that originated in the direction of the experimental cordon and passed the installation on its way to the rendezvous with the *Swiftpack*.

He then checked the mu-rad logs, and found when the ghost signal started getting received and checked its location, supposedly originating in empty space. And sure enough, it lined up to that track as well.

And was transverse.

Whatever that ship was, a Destroyer had made that signal.

He sat back and scratched his jaw. Not only did this ship emit Destroyer-originated mu-rad, but it possessed some of the jendeer stealth technology that had come to humans' rescue the last time the Destroyers had invaded. (The jendeer had stolen the original technology from humans, which Eliyas had had a small part in the creation of; but humans hadn't been able to scale it up beyond a belt for a person to wear. To credit ship-scale stealth field technology to the jendeer was uncomfortable but not wholly inaccurate.) "Ambassador," he called back.

"Yes, Dr. Omarov?"

"I believe that this pirate vessel is, improbably, the ship that the Destroyer ambassadors came in on. We picked up transverse mu-rad coming from nowhere... and this pirate vessel has some highly experimental cloaking technology. I'll keep working on crunching this data, but it's my... speculation—" he cast a quick glance at Iyapo, who smirked —"—that for reasons unknown, they successfully transited from p-space at the expected time four hours ago and remained cloaked. They then rendezvoused with the *Swiftpack*, again for reasons unknown. Ambassador Anderson has some guards with her, yes?"

"*Awk*, a couple, yes, but not military, not marines."

"We might want more reinforcements. That might be the normal crew with Destroyer guests, or it could potentially be a Destroyer boarding party. We have no idea how good-faith they were about wanting to talk."

"We were prepared for that." Krawwkteraak paused.

"But we might have overlooked that more recently in all the excitement going on elsewhere."

"Someone seems to think the usual crew are on there, and didn't broadcast about it until after they'd docked and made sure." Siobhan tapped her screen. "I think we've got some honest-to-God envoys there."

"In any case, the... *Wadja*, was it... is still docked with the *Swiftpack*, so Anderson won't be able to board anyway. I'll update her. She may decide to wait for us to send a second shuttle of reinforcements. I imagine she's trying to talk with whoever's in charge on that ship, but if the pirate vessel is bringing the ambassadors, then I'm sure she will be quite irate with whomever is jeopardizing their delivery."

Iyapo shuddered. "It seems like she's always irate."

"No, Dr. Morgan." Krawwkteraak cocked his head, then pointed one eye straight at Iyapo. "You have not yet seen her irate. Consider yourself fortunate."

"And whoever's screwing around out there, a dead man."

"Quite possibly."

"Weapons fire." Siobhan magnified the image of the *Wadja* and the *Swiftpack*. The former was firing small rounds, aiming at the umbilical. "Looks like the freighter wasn't letting go."

"And the *Wadja* wanted to force the issue." Eliyas nodded in agreement. "The real question is..."

"I believe you humans say, 'eenie-meenie-mynie-moe', *awk*. On which ship are our new friends?"

Chapter XXII

Later investigative accounts would piece together the reality that the Admiral of the 106th Expedition Outside ordered the death of the Historian assigned to the 107th Expedition Outside.

At the time, all I knew was that Blade had told us that a Protector Fleet had followed us.

"This is the Historian of the 107th Expedition Outside, appointed ambassador to the Destroyers. Our status is unknown, but the crew of the *Wadja* have made no explicit threats against us. Please open communications with the Destroyers so that we can avert a diplomatic crisis." That is what I recorded and sent, and what I updated when the Protector fleet started attacking the Destroyers. We received nothing back except for a crude digital signal, which we could not decode at the time but we assumed the Destroyers were sending out to the Protector fleet.

And my message is what Stentorian Blade, having worked his way up to the bridge of the pirate vessel, sternly told me to stop transmitting as it became plausible to assume that Admiral Taut Syndicate of Unclaimed Stars was using the transmission to target us, even though we supposedly should have not appeared on any other instrument readings.

Though we did not have concrete proof, Admiral Taut Syndicate was my first assumption, rather than Admiral Coarse Masonry of a Shattered Well. Porous Kin in particular Recalled the personal politics of Taut Syndicate, and while attacking a Historian was something she could not get away with... we concluded that it was something she would do if she *thought she could* get away with it. As evidenced by the fact that our assumption was later proven, she did not in fact get away with it.

I accompanied the crew of the *Wadja* onto another Destroyer vessel, this one a larger one with apparently minimal crew meant only for cargo transport. Stentorian Blade explained to us that the criminal nature of the *Wadja* precluded it from dropping us off directly, something that we all agreed only exacerbated the breakdown of the situation in local space. But the faster we got on this transport, the faster we could establish contact and hopefully put an end to the conflict before it was too far out of control.

Things seemed to progress as planned, as I followed the crew onto the freighter. There was some trouble getting through the small entryways, but we soon found ourselves in yet another cargo hold, this one larger yet comparatively emptier. The one called Liz was also in the hold with her mixed crew, while the small floating one called Hock and a similar deckhand went into small passageways into which I could not follow.

Unfortunately, the criminal status of the *Wadja* again complicated the proceedings, as it became apparent that Captain Hock and the deckhand had been subdued by the transport's copilot Jenkins, who was actually an officer who had hunted the Destroyer pirate vessel before. Both Jenkins and the *Wadja* were in different places then when they had last dealt with each other, and yet, here they both were.

History moves in cycles.

While I could only understand some of what was being said in the moment, I had made sure to record all of it, and in the interest of the historical record, a more full translation has been provided.

"Crew of the pirate vessel *Wadja*, you are under arrest," said Jenkins.

"Jenkins, this isn't *funny*. I will not be held hostage on my own ship!"

"If you attempt to interfere with my actions, you will be charged as an accessory to piracy, so I suggest you stay there, Captain."

"I can't be *charged* with accessory to piracy *while I am actively being boarded*, you idiot." Captain Lindström released the button on the console and, as an aside, said to Liz, "Thanks for that, by the way."

"I had no idea," said Liz. "Seems smart."

"Someone was charged a few hundred years ago when they let pirates take cargo so there wouldn't be a fight that would harm passengers. Some politician had some vendetta, it was dumb, the captain was acquitted, the law was written."

"Neat." Liz looked around, considering Lieutenant San Martín, her other crew member, and Stentorian Blade, Porous Kin and myself.

Jenkins finally responded, as Lindström reopened the channel from the hold. "Nice trick. We'll stick with the base level interfering with an officer and figure out the rest from there."

"Alright, asshole," said Liz, "what exactly do you want? Congratulations, you've got a couple of blowfish up there, past that you have nothing. I have your Ambassadors here and you're upsetting me, so think very carefully about what you say." She drew one of her ornate pistols and pointed it in my general direction, not bothering to look or aim, but making the point, though it was unclear if Jenkins had any video feed of the hold.

"Elizabeth Bewick, is it? May I call you Liz?"

"You may not."

"Liz." That seemed intentionally rude. "Right now, you're being charged with piracy, which carries a rather stiff sentence. If you harm the Ambassadors, your sentence *will* be death and *will* be carried out summarily." He paused. "That means immediately. By myse—"

"I know what 'summarily' means, you *ass*, do you think I could spend years around Captain Hock Corven without picking up a goddamn thesaurus? Now let me tell you something, Agent, or whatever title you prefer. The sentence for multiple counts of piracy is death. It's a long and arduous process to go through the courts, and there is a big media blowout, and there's arguing, and a delay before the execution, because everybody is oh so *civilized*. So your summary execution actually sounds like a pretty solid alternative." She cocked a lever at the back of her pistol, possibly releasing a safety.

Porous Kin and Stentorian Blade stepped forward, keeping me behind them; Porous Kin could likely take small arms fire from Liz's weaponry for some short amount of time, during which Stentorian Blade would close the distance and disarm Liz, or worse. He did not like fighting, but those descended from the Conquerors were nonetheless quite good at it, and he expected to be so against a species as undersized as those found Outside.

"Ugh. Captain Lindström, will you subdue her already?"

"With *what*, Jenkins? I'm not exactly armed here, and two of the pirates *are*." Liz drew her second pistol and trained it on the captain. "One of them with dual pistols. Flintlocks, if you're interested, all very stereotypical."

Liz mouthed something that looked apologetic, then aloud said, "Captain, please do nothing with your hands aside from keeping that channel open." She then made a motion with the pistol that had been pointed in our direction, drawing it across her throat, while the one pointed at Lindström gestured toward the comm panel. The freighter captain released the button, and Liz said, "Zipzi, I appreciate your initiative, but instead of pointing your gun in my general direction, I want you to see if you can get this hatch open. Got that?"

"Yes, ma'am." The one with the long neck slung his rifle across his back and opened a panel near the hatch, and Liz nodded for Lindström to resume the connection to the cockpit.

"You said three pirates? What happened to the rest?" asked Jenkins.

"They already took their cargo. They're professionals, Jenkins, and have a good sense of timing, unlike a certain recent hire of mine."

"So you don't have all the chips," added Liz. "The *Wadja* could get going and live to pillage another day."

"You don't have the nav package, and more importantly Elizabeth, you do not have your captain. As a matter of fact, they don't have you, either. They have enough supplies to stay cloaked until they starve and go absolutely nowhere. So what you are going to do, is command them to stay attached until I say so. Then they will detach and not go anywhere, under threat of lethal force. It'd be a shame to lose all of that experimental tech that you've gotten running, but... them's the breaks."

Liz growled lightly, clearly trying to formulate a plan of some sort. I sympathized with her plight, but at the same time, she did live a criminal life, and eventually the payment comes due for such a lifestyle.

"Got it," said Zipzi, and the hatch slid open.

"Got what?" said Jenkins. At this point, it was clear that he did not in fact have any sort of visual surveillance of the cargo hold, but was able to ascertain what had happened from Zipzi. Liz must have realized this too, as she glared at him, and he shrunk back.

"Got our ticket out of here," said Liz. "I was just going to take off all quiet-like, but you know what, Agent, I respect you, so I'll tell you what's going to happen. You get to sit up there with my captain, and I get to take your Ambassador back to the *Wadja*. Captain Lindström too, for good measure."

"I must object," said Stentorian Blade, making another step forward, now within claw's reach.

Liz motioned again for Lindström to cut the connection, then said to us, "I am sorry, and I am sure that you all would win in a fight. I'm just... trying to think what Hock would do."

"Is that smart?" said Lieutenant San Martín—Carlos. "He got us into this in the first place. You don't need him. Just... get on the ship. Fly away. Leave them all here."

Liz looked troubled, and considered this. Stentorian Blade crouched low, ready to pounce; Liz snapped both of her weapons at him, as did Zipzi.

"Adding kidnapping to the charges, Ms. Bewick?" asked Jenkins, oblivious to what had transpired over the last few moments in the hold.

"I don't... want to do this," said Liz to us.

"Then don't," implored Carlos. Zipzi swiveled his head back and forth, alarmed; Lindström kept her hand near the panel but otherwise tried to flatten herself against the bulkhead, to keep herself out of the way of whatever was going to happen.

Liz made a face, then nodded again to Lindström, who keyed the panel. "That's the deal. I return the Ambassadors to you when you return Captain Corven to me."

"No can do, Ms. Bewick. Go ahead and take them, but we knew you were here before you dropped your stealth field; we *will* find you again."

"I'll take my chances. Goodbye, Agent." She nodded again, and Lindström again released the button.

"Until we meet again, Ms. Bewick, which will not be as long as you might prefer."

"Ugh, asshole. Okay, everyone stand down, we're not taking anybody. *Wadja*, you read?" She listened for a response. "TIA agent onboard took the Cap'n. I told him I'm going back to the *Wadja* and we're just going to hide for a while. I need you to wait twenty seconds, then detach."

"And what will you do?" asked Lindström. Liz listened to her earpiece, likely fielding a similar question from the bridge of her ship.

Liz looked at us, then at Carlos, then towards the front of the ship. She was clearly weighing her options, against great time pressure.

Finally, she gave a large exhale. "Get the captain, of course."

Chapter XXIII

Admiral Taut Syndicate of Unclaimed Stars was positive that this was not how things were supposed to go.

In her mind, she was to be a vanguard of the Protectors, to finish what had been started centuries ago, to not just punish and isolate these Destroyers, but to annihilate them.

Instead, she had wandered into a trap with what must have been the entirety of the military that these Destroyers could bring to bear. And even then, she would have been able to best them, to win with the righteous virtue that was the right of the Protectors, and the just cause of keeping safe all who live Inside. And yet when she had been on the verge of defeating them, of pushing them back, the treacherous Admiral Coarse Masonry of a Shattered Well betrayed her and ensured her defeat.

What was he after? Did he want the glory of being the one to subdue these Destroyers? But no, that was not his style. He was too weak for that, or so went Taut Syndicate's thinking. No, he actually did want peace with the Destroyers —something that, at best, preserved the disruptive Beat that pervaded this galaxy, and perhaps worse, would not just tear this galaxy apart but enable the Destroyers to spread to other galaxies, to find where more Destroyers would come from and unite—and when their own universe was not enough, to go Inside in their relentless thirst for chaos.

These thoughts can be known with a high degree of accuracy, because Taut Syndicate was not quiet about her beliefs during the battle. Her tirades against the Destroyers and the Admiral of the 107th rattled her bridge officers, likely decreasing their morale and efficiency.

"Admiral, the—the *Beacon of Chrysalism, Spread* is surrendering to the 107th."

"What?!" The Admiral leapt over to the communications officer, and turned up the volume on the console, just in time for two other ships to quickly stand down. "All ships!" she yelled, "Do not relent against this traitor!"

"All Protector vessels of the 106th and 107th," came Coarse Masonry's voice—calmer than Taut Syndicate's, by far. "Cease this infighting. The Historian may yet live. And if they do not, then their death may have been caused by the one who leads you."

"How dare you speak such deception, you—"

"It's no good, Admiral," said the comms officer. "They just targeted our transmitter." He shook his head. "They can't hear us."

"We have managed to recover the existence of a signal sent from an empty point of space. Thank you to the brave crew of your ships who collaborated with us to share this information, as well as discovering that Admiral Taut Syndicate fired on that signal in an attempt to silence it."

Taut Syndicate roared, and punched through the panel with one of her upper claws, then tore it out and threw it across the bridge. "Fabrications! Deceit!"

Elsewhere in the fleet, Coarse Masonry's accusations continued to be heard.

"I take no quarrel with Taut Syndicate's views regarding the Destroyers. I do not agree with those views, but she is not wrong to hold them. If you hold her views, you are not wrong, and I bear you no ill will. I understand how you see things; if you have grown up in this galaxy with the Beat as a daily part of your life, I could not begin to conceive how that might make you feel, and so I understand ill will bore toward them. Even now, they have killed many of us. But do not fire upon them, and for now they will honor this truce while we look into the fate of our Historian.

"So again, I implore you—stand down. Do not provoke them. We will rally together, and we will stand as one before the Destroyers; to meet them in peace, or—if they do in fact bear us ill will of their own—to attack as a unified fleet.

"There are many of you who owe your positions in your fleet to the patronage of Admiral Taut Syndicate. If you stand down now, there will be no repercussions for you. I will not fault you for the actions of the one who led you, *but* —if you continue on your path, and continue to stand in the way of these negotiations—the first we have ever had with any Destroyer civilization, ever, the first chance to understand why isolated Destroyer civilizations keep attacking us, injuring the Breath, issuing their Cries—if you stand in the way of this moment of epiphany of which we are within claw's reach, then you will meet the same justice as that which will soon meet Taut Syndicate."

Across the tattered remains of the 106th Expedition Outside, some ships ceased fire; others kept firing on the 107th; and two decided to meet their fate, charging into the regrouped fleet of the Destroyers, and quickly met their end.

Onboard the flagship, an even more discordant scene played out. Admiral Taut Syndicate commanded her crew to continue firing on the 107th, intent now on bringing down its own flagship, inferior to her own. But Taut Syndicate's ship had been fighting this whole time, been the focus of many attacks, and was in dire need of repair and resupply.

Its crew were not in much better shape. While the Admiral was breaking down, the lead gunnery officer and the engineer coordinator silently looked to each other, nodded, then stood to challenge Taut Syndicate. She saw their challenge, and met them head-on. It had been a long time since those descended from the Conquerors had fought in such a terrible manner, and much hardware on the ship was destroyed during the fight, but in the end, Taut Syndicate emerged victorious.

"Remove these from my sight," she said. The fight seemed to have calmed her down, focused her. Two security officers moved to comply. "No. On second thought—they stay there. This is what happens when my orders are disobeyed."

She returned to the dais at the center of the bridge, struck a display screen to coax it to life, and consulted her crew roster. "Please send up Gunner Deft Caress in the Velvet Constellation and Engineer Fate Encountered on the Garden Path to take over their predecessors' stations."

The ship continued to rock as the flagships traded fire. Larger than any vessel present, it could soak up much damage, and in fact would continue to do so as the combined efforts of the 107th Expedition Outside and the fleet of the Destroyers focused on it. It could only last so long, and Taut Syndicate's bridge crew wondered what she had planned. Escape? To go down in a blaze of glory? Many were worried, but everyone—everyone left—would stand by her decision.

The two new bridge officers entered the bridge—one of whom was the gunner with whom Taut Syndicate had exchanged covert messages earlier in the battle. Deft Caress marched up to Taut Syndicate and saluted, upper claws crossed downwards above his head. She returned his salute and motioned to the gunnery console, then turned back to what she was doing.

Deft Caress dispassionately looked at the console, then at the two corpses on the deck. Then, he turned to Taut Syndicate, and speared her through her carapace with both of his claws.

Not expecting her loyal crewmember—the erstwhile assassin, her right-claw man to whom she had entrusted the execution of her own act of treachery—to be, in his own way, treacherous, Taut Syndicate only had time for a surprised gasp before succumbing to death.

Deft Caress took her place and drew himself to his full height. "Cease firing. Power down all external lights so the Destroyers know we are standing down. Signal the 106th. Tell them this: our Admiral led us well, but her time, and the time for her way of thinking, is over."

Chapter 24

"This is stupid!" hissed Carlos.

"Carlos," Liz whispered back, "lesson number one—loyalty. I am loyal to the captain, so I go get the captain; and you are loyal to me, so you shut the fuck up and listen to orders." She shifted her ankle, trying to relieve the pressure, but it was tough with Carlos so close.

"I did plenty of that in TOD, kinda thought you were all above that stuff."

"The decision-making *discussion* was totally democratic. Then I decided and that's when you started *shutting the fuck up*." He started to object again but she squirmed an arm up and covered his mouth. She listened, and heard footsteps approaching on the rattling metal grating of the floor, and shoved Carlos' face back for good measure to make sure he was paying attention too.

Jenkins approached slowly. As he got closer, Liz could see that he had a rather large stun gun drawn. The boxy weapon was tucked under one arm, yellow paint chipped away and only a few traces remained of where Liz knew black embellishments should be. She'd had the fortune, or misfortune, to have taken hits from such a device at two separate times in her career, and only one was consensually. She rather doubted that Jenkins had the power dial turned that low at this moment.

She focused on holding her breath, Carlos' mouth, and a pistol; and after what seemed like an eternity, Jenkins walked past them, none the wiser. She slowly released her hold on the first two, but kept her pistol close. She waited another moment, then whispered to Carlos, "Would you be so kind?"

Carlos popped a latch, and they both quietly tumbled out of the locker they'd been hiding in for the last ten minutes.

Liz tried again to shake out her ankle, and winced as pins and needles raced up her leg. She started limping forward, the way Jenkins had come. As she went, she kept an ear out for Carlos as he followed, frustrated that she couldn't trust him fully and had to keep some of her attention on him. She almost wished she'd taken Zipzi with her instead, but with the question of who to leave with Lindström and the Destroyers, she trusted Carlos *far* less.

The *Swiftpack* was a large ship—certainly bigger than the *Wadja*—but not in a way that would take Jenkins a long time to search. Its rear was mostly taken up by the large, unobstructed and mostly empty cargo hold, while the smaller front section was largely comprised of the two-seat flight deck and the half-dozen compartments making up the meager living quarters. It wouldn't take long to get to where Jenkins had ambushed her captain and crewmate, but they also wouldn't have long before Jenkins started making his way back up.

Liz approached the hatch to the flight deck, and braced herself for the worst. The hatch slid open, and she looked to the floor, hoping to see a pair of peacefully resting kikan on the ground, fearing to instead see blood and death. Instead, she saw... nothing. She looked up just as she heard a choked-off laugh from behind her, and jumped back—Hock and Dekk had both puffed fully and were softly bouncing against the ceiling. She shook her head and stepped into the flight deck, trying to slap Hock awake.

Carlos stepped in as well, and shut the door behind them. Liz cast him a mistrustful glance, and he said, "When he comes back, it's better that he doesn't see all of us through the hatch."

Liz nodded wordlessly, and wondered if she was being too harsh on him. He could have given her away in the locker, and that would have ended this rescue mission. (Then again, he might have refrained because her pistol had been pointed in the general vicinity of his crotch.) He also could have tried to trap Liz with Dekk and Hock in the flight deck (but then he might not have done so because that would leave her with full control of the ship, including possibly life support). He was smart, and maybe loyal to her, and *maybe* maybe loyal to the captain, but there was too much uncertainty to be sure from which set of virtues—intelligence and patience, or loyalty and solidarity—had resulted in the choices he'd made so far.

"Hubzhuh?" moaned Hock as he slowly woke up. He deflated slowly and stabilized at eye level and glanced around, taking in who was—and wasn't—present. "Oh, that—you know, I had him! Where is—!"

Liz rolled her eyes and slapped her hand over his mouth; it was getting a lot of use for that purpose today. "He's checking out the hold," she said to him quietly. She took her hand off Hock's mouth and started smacking Dekk around. "If he's thorough, we have maybe five minutes. Did Dekk finish what he was doing?"

"Yes'm, I found the wool in the water drawer," Dekk

replied. Liz just stared at him, then hit him once, harder. "Ow!"

"Did. You. Get the nav data?"

"I, uh. Where... oh! Uh, hold on, ma'am, everything's kinda fuzzy." Dekk deflated and dropped down to the panel in the copilot's chair, trying to jog his memory. "No... I was looking through the files in their directory when he hit the cap'n. He took my workstation away, too. So, uh... not sure how we'll take it home?"

"Just load it up. Can you patch it into the comm array?"

"Uhhh... sure, that should work. Give me a minute. Um. Should I be worried about this?"

Liz looked around him at the panel, where it was signaling an incoming transmission request. "Ignore it," she advised. "We'll be out of here soon enough." Dekk bobbed in acknowledgment and set to work.

"Hey-hey, you're doing well." Hock bopped against Liz's shoulder. "Decided not to leave me after all?"

"There was a fully democratic decision-making process, then I made a decision," she said, looking at Carlos. He held up his hands in a gesture of innocence. "Did you think I was going to?"

"Didn't really have time to think about it while I was knocked out. Then when I woke up I realized you'd passed up a perfectly good opportunity at getting yourself command of a ship."

"What, the *Wadja*? Nooo thank you."

"Hey, what's wrong with the *Wadja*?!"

"I just figured I'd get you back to your ship, and I'd take this one. Gotta think of a new name for her, though, what do you think of the *Black Plank*?"

"That's an awful name, and now I know you're bluffing." Hock wrapped a fin around Liz. "Thanks for coming for me."

She hugged him back. "Always."

"Found it," said Dekk. "Nice little program sitting here, plus a bigger database. Uh, probably too long to send it all in one go without any signal deterioration taking out chunks."

"Just repeat it a bunch and hopefully we can repair it." Liz keyed her earpiece. "*Wadja*, you out there?"

Static answered with just enough definition that using her imagination, Liz could pick out Fovak's voice saying, "Yes, ma'am." Liz couldn't quite resist the urge to look out the viewport for the *Wadja*, but her attempt was naturally fruitless while the pirate ship's stealth field was active.

"Be ready to receive on this channel, data burst. Say again, data burst on this channel. But first—Zipzi, you good?"

The thurffe's voice came back very quietly. "All good."

"Okay. Turn your volume down, we're broadcasting using the ship's arrays on this channel."

"Got it."

"Good. *Wadja*, ready to receive data burst?"

"Data burst, ready to receive," she could faintly pick out. She turned her own earpiece down to minimum, then nodded at Dekk. He punched in a few commands on the console and pulled a somewhat impressive-looking lever. A bouquet of white noise filled Liz's ear.

"This isn't encrypted, you know," Dekk said.

"That's fine. Everybody else in the system has the clearance for this software. We're the only ones... uh, pirating it."

"You're terrible."

"Love you too, Dekk."

"Hate to break it up," said Carlos, clearly not hating doing so, "but if Jenkins hasn't found Zipzi yet, he's probably on his way up."

Liz shrugged one shoulder, and when she dropped it she

slipped her second pistol out of its holster. "He got the drop on these two because of the element of surprise. The thing is, now we know that he's coming, we know that he's armed with a stun gun—"

"A what? He just took us out with his fists. I sometimes forget how strong your species is. You're so... spindly."

"Thanks Dekk. Yeah, he grabbed a stun gun from somewhere on the way back to the hold. I can't help but notice that neither of you are armed. Carlos, you have your pistol, still?"

"Right here." He held it up in front of himself.

"Good, said Hock. "Three guns to his one, I like those odds. We'll wait here and ambush him instead of letting him somehow slip around behind us. Carlos, could you listen for when the good copilot is making his way back here?"

"Roger, Captain." He leaned against the hatch with his left ear, his pistol in his right hand.

"Signal's repeating," said Dekk. "I'd wanna get at least two more full broadcasts before I'm confident the *Wadja* will be able to reconstruct the program."

"We'll get you that time," Liz promised. She sat down at the captain's chair and did a quick check of available systems. "I'm going to guess that if there was a way to track people through the ship, Jenkins would've used it already. Do we have anything else?"

"Check for door locks," said Hock, peering over her shoulder.

"Probably not," said Carlos, "I've got a manual lock right here." He patted a chunky red lever with white stripes (Liz had forgotten just how chunky *everything* was on human-designed ships).

"And the cabin's not really big enough to use hatches as atmo containment if there's a breach." She reached over to the copilot's chair that Dekk was hovering above and removed the seat cushion, finding an environment suit stashed under it. "If they have an emergency, looks like they just throw a suit on."

"I doubt they have any in my size, so let's not go blowing any holes in the, ah, *Black Plank*, shall we?"

"Ugh."

"You named it."

"And I don't plan on keeping it. I meant what I said, Hock, we are not taking this ship. We're taking what we need then getting back to the *Wadja*. I don't want to screw with delivering the ambassadors any more than you already have."

"...Fair enough. We'll find a *Black Plank* for you some other time."

"Maybe I'll invite Lindström, I bet she can hang."

"He's here!" hissed Carlos, and the hatch slid open. Jenkins stood on the other side, momentarily stunned at everyone's presence, then brought his stun gun up to bear. Liz pointed both of her pistols at him, and Carlos held up his one in a very military two-handed grip.

"Hey-hey, three to one," said Hock jovially. "And yours is a stunner that could inconvenience us at worst. Now, I have a deep, abiding respect for..." He trailed off, then glanced aside at Liz for help.

"An agent of the Terran Intelligence Agency," she supplied.

"Yes, for one of those. And I have respect for the charges you'd add to my rap sheet if I killed one of you, let me tell you! So why don't you just set that down, yes?"

At Hock's proposal, five things happened in rapid succession.

First, Jenkins made quick eye contact with Carlos.

Second, Carlos started to swing his pistol towards Liz.

Third, Liz—whose second pistol had been trained

somewhere between the two of them—snapped said pistol to Carlos and his hands as they came around.

Fourth, Liz fired said pistol.

Fifth, Carlos screamed.

Liz kept her gun on him for an extra moment as he slumped to the deck, cradling his ruined hands and wailing in pain, then brought her second pistol back to Jenkins. The intelligence agent was too surprised at his three-way standoff being interrupted to get any sort of initiative on Liz, and when he looked back to her, the primary expression on his face was "bewildered". Liz tilted her head to the side and considered him.

"That face, Agent Jenkins, means that my dear first mate here is considering visiting similar violence upon your own person. If you value your wonderfully dextrous human hands, I would set that stun gun down on the deck with the muzzle facing yourself and slide it towards us."

Jenkins nodded slowly, common sense finally winning out among his various other impulses, and he started to comply.

"You... you *bitch!*" said Carlos from his position on the deck, leaning against a bulkhead for support—his first coherent words since underestimating Liz's resolve. "You could have just... taken all you wanted, but no, you had to play the f-*fucking* hero, and you made me—"

A loud sound somewhere between a buzz and a low-frequency sine wave erupted, and Jenkins, who had been holding the stun gun with the muzzle to the side, continued rotating it and lowered it the rest of the way to the grating, touching down about the same time Carlos' torso hit the deck as well.

"Agent Jenkins," said Liz, "you have my sincere gratitude for your cooperation and initiative."

"How?" he asked as if in reply, and stood back up

slowly, hands in the air, using the tip of his boot to kick the stun gun towards the pirates.

"Mr. San Martín is not deaf. He had far more advance warning that you were on the way than he actually filled us in on. I don't know exactly what his endgame was—probably helping you arrest us—but he overplayed his hand." Liz winced and tried not to look at the ends of Carlos' arms.

"Too soon, Liz," said Hock, clearly trying to suppress a laugh. "Dekk, did the third transmission start?"

"Just ended." Liz belatedly realized that she wasn't getting the white noise through her earpiece anymore. "I, um, didn't want to interrupt."

"Excellent, and I commend your discretion. *Wadja?*"

"Good to hear your voice, Captain," said Fovak faintly but more clearly than before; they'd likely drifted closer in the meantime.

"Good to hear yours. You get the package?"

"Recompiling now. Looks intact. Going to be, uh, kinda scary to use it at first."

"If it's any consolation, even if it works perfectly, we're apparently still jumping through a parallel universe and pissing off big scary aliens, so I wouldn't worry about it."

"You have a way of putting things in perspective, Captain Corven."

"I do, don't I?"

"Speaking of perspective, check your scopes, there's a shuttle coming in that'll be here in a couple minutes."

"I see it," said Liz, adjusting her earpiece's volume back to normal while keeping a pistol on Jenkins. "Must be what that incoming hail was all about. *Wadja*, your umbilical's still intact?"

"Sure is, we shot the *Swiftpack's* to shit but we're still good."

"I think you mean the *Blac—*"

Liz smacked Hock, and he bounced off the viewport. "Copy that. Dekk, stay here, make sure the *Swiftpack* registers a good seal when they connect up. I'm going to check on the ambassadors and the captain."

"But didn't... oh."

"Yeah. Sorry, Agent. They were in the cargo container the whooooole time."

"Damn."

Liz holstered her pistols and picked up the stun gun. "I'd ask if you would promise to be good with my two friends up here, but..."

Jenkins shook his head. "No, I get it. Well played." He narrowed his eyes. "Both of you. Ms. Bewick, I hope it's not forward of me to expect you to be captaining your own ship sooner rather than later; no offense, Captain Corven, but when it comes time for me to update TIA's threat assessments, I'm more worried about your first mate here."

"Aw, my first personal compliment from the law." She fired the stun gun at Jenkins, and as he twitched and slumped to the deck, she mused, "I think I'll remember this day forever."

Chapter Twenty-Five

Eliyas slumped back onto the sofa. "Well. That's that."

"Seems like," said Siobhan. She held off on joining Eliyas and instead made for Iyapo's liquor cabinet. "Can I get you something?"

"I'm good." Eliyas closed his eyes and rubbed a hand along the bridge of his nose. "I told Iyapo I'd relieve him in four hours and I'd rather not be hung over."

"I wasn't asking if you wanted to get trashed."

"And yet I know there's a bottle of Azure Zinfandel in there that has my name on it and I'm not sure I'd have the energy to practice restraint with it."

Siobhan furrowed her brow then ducked down, and Eliyas heard the sound of glass bottles clinking against each other. "Huh," came her voice, muffled by the cabinet she was looking into, "so there is, though I don't actually see your name on the bottle."

"Do you know anybody else that likes thurffe blue wines?"

"I've never known a human to touch blue wine, no."

"Ergo, mine."

"Fair. I'll just keep it here for now, then, and when we have our party I'll bring it along for you."

Eliyas groaned and leaned his head back against the sofa. "Party?"

Siobhan stood back up, holding a bottle of whiskey and grabbing a glass. "Yes, party. We did it, Eliyas. Oh, don't give me that," she said in response to his sidelong glare, "I know we're not done with the actual science of it. But we know the basic nature of mu-rad, we know the basics of subspace travel, we know—in the broadest of terms—what the Destroyers are."

"I don't know how you can claim we know the basics of subspace travel. We haven't even proven the actual mechanism, just that p-space is involved."

"Okay, fine, though whatever these 'chains' are that they keep talking about, it sounds like it may as well be wormhole theory, or close enough to it as to be indistinguishable." She sat down at an armchair across from Eliyas and set her glass on the table, and poured herself a measure of the drink she'd pilfered from Iyapo's stocks. "And now it's looking like there's some peace accords to be had. They just sent out a request for a more robust diplomatic support team on the last interval, so pretty soon we won't need to play control center to Krawwkteraak and whoever else.

"We did it. There's more to do on the *exact* mechanism of travel, and we've opened up some brand-new sciences that future generations of baby physicists will be able to devote their whole lives to, so of course we're not *done*, but when that diplomatic team gets here?" She lifted her glass to Eliyas. "The Alpha Point science team gets a well deserved break, a solid eight hours of sleep, and a God damn day off."

"Ugh, that sounds like heaven."

"Hence, party."

"That does not sound like heaven."

"I'm not talking about some undergrad rager, you idiot. Ji-min's throwing a low-key social gathering together in the mess, maybe putting up whatever decorations they can get their hands on. I'm talking drinks, music, talking to people about stuff that isn't work."

"I don't see the appeal."

Siobhan cast him a withering glare. "Admit it. You don't have to say that you like people more, but I *know* you *dislike* them less than you used to."

He made a show of weighing the options, rocking his head back and forth while he was still looking at the ceiling. "I might, with more sleep and with a glass of wine, make such an allowance."

"I'll take it."

They sat in silence for what seemed like a few minutes, each thinking of how the last few months had gone—from learning an outdated theory of subspace to discovering a whole new parallel universe, full of different physics and other mysteries. From working on a problem for the betterment of science (and allowing for economic growth and other such soft ideas) to initiating diplomatic relations (another soft idea, but one worth pursuing) with an ancient civilization that had a history of making war on the species of the galaxy. It had, indeed, been an eventful few months.

"Eliyas. Wake up." He snapped his head off the back of the sofa, blinking away the crud that had settled in his eyelids.

"I'm fine," he said, and gratefully took the glass of water that Siobhan held out for him.

"I'd hope so. You've had a good three-hour nap." Oh. "Figured you wouldn't mind the wake-up call to relieve Iyapo."

"Oh. Thanks." He downed the water and stood,

stretching; his mind hadn't noticed the lapse but his body, particularly his neck, was well aware of the time spent asleep sitting up on the sofa.

"Unless you want me to take this next shift," offered Siobhan, still sitting and clearly hoping he wouldn't take her up on the offer.

"No, that's fine," he said. "Take over for me in four hours. By the time your shift's done, that'll be... two intervals since the diplomatic team sent for backup. They should have crew coming in on that interval."

"Yep. Then eight hours, then party," she said with a smirk.

"Dr. Doyle... Siobhan..."

"Listen." She stood up in front of him and made to take his hands in hers, then thought better of it. "I'm not asking you to become some social butterfly. Just... enjoy a glass or two of your wine, and try to keep from looking pissed off and scaring people away from you. Bring a book or something, the worst that happens is you get some reading done."

"The worst that could happen would be if I had a good time and enjoyed myself." He smiled slightly despite himself.

"Heaven forbid." Siobhan reached out again, and this time finally clasped his upper arms. He made no attempt to shrug her off. "It's not an order or anything, but it's a request, and it would mean a lot to me if you were there," she said. "And if you don't do Ji-min's big shindig, then... at least join me and Iyapo back here afterward? We just started watching *Ashfall*, I think you'd like it." She released his shoulders and stepped back.

"Is that the drama about the pirate captain that tries going legit but gets blackmailed into being the front operation of a worse pirate?"

"Oh, you've seen it?"

"I could tell you how it ends if you want."

Siobhan rapidly closed the distance again, thrusting a finger in Eliyas' face. *"Don't you dare."*

Eliyas laughed. "I got curious and looked it up on the network. Read the synopsis."

"That's cheating."

"Looked kind of interesting but I didn't have the time for it."

"Well. If you'd like to make the time..."

"And start midway through the season? I would just be lost. Sounds awful, really." He let that hang for a moment as Siobhan tried not to look crestfallen. "No, I'm afraid I must simply insist on imposing upon you to start over from the pilot."

She smiled. "Dr. Omarov, you really are a terrible individual."

"I know. So terrible that I may stay at the party longer than expected and force you and Dr. Morgan to wait for me. Truly the worst kind of person."

"Truly," she said, laughing. "I look forward to it."

Eliyas thought for a moment, then nodded. "You know what? Me too."

Chapter XXVI

When we saw Liz open the door of the cargo container, it felt like a new day.

The reasons for this were many. Liz herself seemed to be moving more freely; I did not know human physiology well at the time, but there were things I picked up on, and this was perhaps the only time I ever saw her "loosened up", as I would later learn the term to be. She did not have the stress of being a captive, nor of clandestinely trying to deliver us while getting away herself, nor of Jenkins' actions working contrary to her own. She also did not seem overly burdened by Carlos San Martín's absence. I wish that I could have asked her about all of this, but time was short.

Perhaps that feeling of a fresh start was because she told us that she would soon depart, and that the ambassadors for their kind would soon be there. We would soon be fulfilling our purpose Outside, and working to create an accord that would benefit both of our societies.

Or maybe, it is because the cargo container had been rather stuffy and dark, and we were all quite glad to have been released from it.

For an unknown span of time, the mostly-full container had, in addition to its stated manifest, also played host to myself, Stentorian Blade of Songs in Bloom, and Porous Kin, Waking From Ignorance; as well as the pirate Zipzi and the freighter captain Åsa Lindström. Stentorian Blade and Lindström were able to easily climb to nooks higher in the container, while Zipzi and I concealed ourselves behind Porous Kin, who, from the right angle, vaguely resembled a stack of the smaller crates within the container.

Jenkins had arrived, as Liz had predicted, and methodically looked around the cargo hold. We could hear him searching, as his footsteps occasionally echoed through the surface of the hold and up through the container. He did check the container itself, but only cursorily, at the end, when he had apparently seemed convinced that Liz had followed through on her stated intention to abscond with all of us back to her ship.

We decided to wait longer, in case Jenkins for some reason returned, but when the time came for someone to release us, it was in fact Liz.

As we emerged from the container, she offered her farewells, as she was to leave and the Destroyer—no, the Outsider ambassadors would soon arrive in her stead. To Lindström, she offered "Mr. San Martín's former position". The freighter captain seemed to consider this, then declined, stating that she wanted to see us safely delivered. Liz nodded, then said, "The offer remains open. There's a bar on Femrehsser Station in the Trappist station, if you want to meet me for a drink in a month."

Lindström looked Liz up and down, and then said, "I'll consider it. I always thought I might look good in a longcoat."

Liz quickly closed and opened one of her eyes. "I promise, you will." She then turned to us and told us that she wished she could stay, and I assured her that we understood why she couldn't. I told her that we could not wish her good fortune, but we could wish her good health, and she seemed pleased with that. "May you enjoy both," she said to us, then departed from the ship with Zipzi.

Lindström made some attempts to be a good host, but the three of us were happy to simply wait in the hold as we heard the sounds of the *Wadja's* departure reverberate through the hull, then a scant few moments later, similar sounds as the shuttle docked.

There is not much to say from this point forward. We met the ambassadors and, upon discovering our stature, they elected to bring the freighter to the installation rather than host us on their own shuttle. A shuttle from the Protector fleets also met us at the installation, with Admiral Coarse Masonry of a Shattered Well and the Historian that had been assigned to the 106th.

We learned things that would be more properly covered in the history that that Historian would Tell—of Coarse Masonry's self-appointment as military envoy who would, within the structure of the deal we created, work with Outsider military to ensure everyone's safety as travel between universes might become more common. We learned of Admiral Taut Syndicate's attempt to disrupt any chance of peace talks, including preliminary analysis of onboard security systems that suggested she may have attempted to have us killed, which agreed with our own observations. And we learned of her fall to her own assassin, Deft Caress. What had caused him to commit such an act? Did he seek power; did he seek to salve his own guilt at perhaps having killed us; did he see an opportunity; was he afraid for his life if the flagship had continued participating in the battle. Something that would bother the three of us for some time is, did he intentionally miss us when firing upon us? We could not be sure of the answers to any of these questions at the time, and would have to wait for his trial; and for the history of those events to be Told to the College of History, then back to us for Porous Kin to learn and be able to Recall in the future.

Stentorian Blade offered to Tell the Historian of our own experience, and while he did share what we knew from our perspective while potentially being targeted by Taut Syndicate—as such events intersected with the history of the events on the flagship of the 106th—their Teller stated that otherwise, the events we had witnessed were ours. We had Observed, and we would Tell. We would write our history, and it would be verified through what resources could be used to do so, then we would submit our history to the College of History, a first-person account of a rare occasion when a Historian themselves had been an important figure.

From that moment forward, however—the talks, and all that came afterward—our story would be Observed and Told by the Historian of the 106th, now formally assigned to Observe the events that we participated in.

Much will be spoken and written of the revelations, of the Outsiders' lack of ill intent, of their ignorance of us and what their method of travel had done to us, and what that might mean for the other times we had waged war on Outsiders in the past; but perhaps most so of the Breath, and their newcomer's perspective of it. What is learned will reverberate not just in our own culture, but in their own. As Outsiders who have not known the Breath as natively as we, they may only see it as another natural emission; but some will hear, and some will know, and some will follow in the footsteps of those who use it not just for science, but to enrich themselves. Their universe may not be alive, as ours is; but *they are*, all the same, and they will carry the Breath with them.

We are not sure what we will do after the talks. We study the past, not the future. We cannot foresee what the universe—universes—will be like. There will certainly always be a place for Historians. But, it seems, there may also always be a place for ambassadors, for first contact specialists. For people that can be comfortable in either universe, and among the people of either universe.

We do not know what history has in store for us. But for a time, at least, we were not passive accessories to it but active participants. And perhaps, to have been participants in the creation of one great moment... that would be enough.

But then, we can never be *certain* that history is done with us. Some time from now—a year, a decade, a century—we might be called upon again, to be in the right place at the right time to make great things happen.

After all, history moves in cycles.

Epilogue

Åsa Lindström sat in the Feathers Retreat and wondered again what she was doing. This was the third bar in the station—out of at least a dozen drinking establishments—that she'd tried, and so far had found success only in mispronouncing local beers and wondering how long was long enough to lurk in a place to try to find Liz.

This was stupid, of course, and every bar she didn't find Liz in was another chance to just head back to the *Swiftpack* and put this whole business behind her.

But she was ready for a career change, and after seeing how she'd been used by a government agent (ignored on her ship, made to sit idly by and watch while Jenkins ignored the big picture for a small, personal victory), maybe being on the side of the law wasn't all it was cracked up to be.

Then again, piracy wasn't a nice, clean lifestyle choice either. Sure, Liz and Captain Corven had been transporting the ambassadors to her and that was all good and altruistic, but their possession of stealth field technology as well as a working subspace drive meant that they'd obviously stolen it from *somewhere* and at this point it was a foregone conclusion that it was the *Wadja* that had boarded the *Exo Sovlin Hygiea* and taken that same cargo from Captain Ramesh Sampradja. And sure, Ramesh was a prick who deserved to be humiliated, but that was just another day for the pirates. They did that all the time. Could Åsa do that?

She could try, find out. If it didn't work... well, if it didn't work, there would be no easy retirement. The best she could hope for was to get arrested and a lesser sentence by helping them find the *Wadja*.

Ugh, but that would probably have her working with Jenkins again.

And so it went, her thoughts spinning around and around, such that when she turned to vacate her stool at the bar she ran into someone and spilled what was left of her drink all over that someone's business suit. "Hey!" the someone shouted, and Åsa found that the someone—in addition to the soaked suit—possessed a human woman's face, long hair in a severe bun, and a scowl.

"Sorry," Åsa mumbled. "I didn't—can I pay for your drink, to apologize?"

"Hmph. Eric, my usual. She'll bring it to me. Make sure she doesn't try anything funny with it." Without making eye contact, she turned and strutted back to her corner table.

The bartender set a glass on the table and filled it with a few different liquids, none of which (aside from pineapple juice) Åsa was quite sure she recognized. "Better do as she says," the bartender said with a half shrug, and went back to serving others.

It's this behavior by suits that makes me want to quit in the first place. She brought the drink to the woman's table and set it in front of her. "Very sorry, again. Have a good-"

"Have a seat, Captain." The woman picked up her glass and took a sip, trying to cover a smile.

Åsa slowly sat, studying the woman, and suddenly it clicked. "It's you! Li—um."

"Let's go with Eliza," Liz said, and extended her hand, which Åsa shook. "Sorry about all of that. And also, you know." She gestured to what she was wearing. "All of this." She fiddled with the bun. "People tend to look for the hat."

"You know, now that I look, your makeup does seem a bit understated for the average Trappist businesswoman."

"No points for playing detective after you know the answer." She lounged back into the booth.

Åsa put her hands up. "You got me."

"I didn't expect to see you," Liz said.

"I didn't know if I'd come either. Still thinking about it."

"I mean, you've got a pretty sweet gig already. Freighter captain. Making the legit bucks."

"Sure. At the beck and call of the people who wear suits —uh, no offense, I think—and apparently at the whims of spooks too. It's all a bit... tarnished?"

"Captain Lindström—"

"Please. It's... it's Åsa. I mean, technically still a captain. Could walk out of here, go back to that. Just, doesn't feel right for you to call me that."

"Alright. Åsa, disillusionment with otherwise perfectly fine employment does not automatically make you cut out for... my line of work. Now, mind you, deciding on our... marks... *is* a democratic process, but you can't be squeamish. Same goes for if it comes to resistance. If someone gets in our way, we... get them out of the way. Violently."

"How many people have you... gotten out of the way?"

Liz scratched her cheek nervously. "I, uh, try not to keep count. Let's say under a dozen, plus a couple dozen more with disfiguring injuries. All of them people who were trying to do the same or worse to me first, mind you."

"Fair. And I mean, you stunned Jenkins."

"Stun guns are great, but they don't have the range or accuracy, or—frankly—shock value."

"No, I'm saying, I might've wanted to take his ear or something."

"Okay, so willing to get your hands dirty, check." Liz took another sip. "The position's yours, Åsa, if you'd like to take it."

"Who would my direct report be?"

"Your direct report! Hoo boy, we'll break you of that, don't you worry. I'm taking you on as my assistant, you do what I say, you do as the Captain says. I'm sure with your experience you'll pick up the job in no time."

"Oh, I knew I'd forgotten my résumé."

"No worries, I looked into it. A bit surprised you're still captaining freighters, I thought they'd've promoted you by now."

"They'll either promote me to an office job or keep treating me like dirt. Or both, actually. I like the stars. I'll stay on a ship as long as I can."

Liz nodded and stood up, finished with her drink. "Speaking of ships... did you bring one with you? That's a nice start to your employment."

"I thought about that." Åsa followed the other women out of the bar. "The only one I've got access to is the *Swiftpack*. It's here, but... that's a bit recognizable, at this point. Dare I say historic. Not a good one to lay low in."

"Ah, but we could hock it to a museum for a pretty penny. And can I be honest? When Hock asked if we should take it, got us in a bit of a mess? Stupid idea, it'd be awful for our line or work."

"That too. Shame. But hey, I think the drive is modular enough to take and store away until you can install it on something else." She shrugged. "You seem to have figured it out before."

Liz laughed. "That we did. So I take it you accept?"

Åsa stopped, considering, and looked up and down the concourse. People milled past, going about their lives, most just trying to get by, not really working for themselves. Not living up to their potential, many of them not even given the chance.

Åsa Lindström still didn't know if the pirate's life was for her. But she recognized that she was at a crossroads. She knew the path ahead would be dangerous, and continuing down it would be a clean break. She wouldn't be able to go back—behind her would be places and people she had known all her life, no longer welcome to her. But in front of her... a new life, new places and new people, a new world ready to welcome her. And in Liz, a mentor and a guide to get her there.

"Yeah. Yeah, I accept." She paused for a moment and considered Liz's attire. "Now. Do you know any good places around here to get a longcoat?"

THE TREASON

DUOLOGY

Preface:
How We Stopped the Destroyers, the Treason Duology, and what Reddit has to do with all of this

How We Stopped the Destroyers gets its roots in the r/HFY subbreddit—a community on Reddit (full name: "Humanity, Fuck Yeah!") focused on writing, originating with "Humans Are Weird" style fiction on Tumblr. This is to say, it started online.

I was introduced to r/HFY in late 2021, particularly to the story *A job for a deathworlder* by Lanzen Jars. I began to read more, wondered if I had anything to contribute, and workshopped some ideas, but none ever had the spark that would make it interesting enough to write, let alone read.

Then one night, my subconscious mind—having been flooded with new tropes and ideas to add to the space opera miasma it had grown up in—decided to dream about a human stealing technology from aliens, and then escaping from the space station while driving a Hyundai Kona.

I woke up, and tried my best to commit the details to memory, and over the course of the day drafted, "What's Treason Between Friends?" I posted it at the end of the day, having taken out some of the more absurd elements and added a second half where the stolen technology pays off.

The story was well received, and I then, over the course of the next week, wrote a follow-up, "Mutual Treason", exploring the same events from the opposite point of view. I did this in my novella *Firestorm*, and it's a method of storytelling that I greatly enjoy exploring.

And so, both entries having been enjoyed by many (though by no means blowing up the subreddit or becoming staples, the first one did at least make the Featured Content list for February 2022), that naturally meant that I was done writing. The Destroyers had been introduced and rebuffed, but surely there wasn't anything more to them worth exploring, right?

Right?

I started work on *How We Stopped the Destroyers* soon after.

The plan was always to write the story in its entirety, then to serialize; then, as I realized how much fun I was having, I knew that I wanted to self-publish the paperback, my first since *Firestorm* ten years ago. (That book will likely be getting a fresh coat of paint for a second edition after this one is published.)

The two short stories included here both differ slightly from their original incarnations. While writing the second story, I realized some oversights from the first, and I wanted to make a few changes so it would dovetail better into the second story. Also worth noting is that on Reddit, "destroyers" was lowercase as a species name (same as human, jendeer, shiwiik), whereas in *Destroyers* it was capitalized to, well, "Destroyers", as it's more of a proper noun, so I've also made that change here as well.

As of publication, the original story posts, as well as the original serialization of *How We Stopped the Destroyers*, can still be read at r/HFY, easily gathered at my author wiki page: https://www.reddit.com/r/hfy/wiki/authors/boterbug/

What's Treason Between Friends?

Cassidy stood stock still, not daring to move while Xynka scanned the room. In front of a human, Cass could dance a jig while wearing the stealth field generator and the only giveaway would be the out of tempo staccato of two left feet. Theoretically, it was perfect. But the thing about state secrets that other species aren't supposed to know about, is that there's no way to test in a lab if a jendeer's superior eyesight could detect the stealth field. And that left field tests.

Field test, of course, made it sound like a more controlled situation than it was. What had happened in reality was that a transmission came in for Xynka that Cass hadn't been unable to immediately decode, and then he had left his quarters with speed. She didn't need to decode the message itself to know what it said—if the encryption was so new that she couldn't crack it, and for Xynka to leave immediately, meant that their friendly rivalry had come to an end. The jendeer had, somehow, found out about stealth field technology, and now Xynka was coming for it.

The timing of that message was, of course, either unlucky or fortuitous, but either way was suspicious; just this morning, Cass had received a similar, new-encryption, highest-security message from the Terran Intelligence Agency, informing her that the opportunity had come to get humanity's own holy grail—blueprints for the subspace jump technology that had allowed the Jendeeri Stellar Economic Union to keep its stranglehold on commerce in known space.

Cassidy held her breath, waiting for her opportunity. Though the jendeer had famously acute eyesight, their hearing and smell were pretty terrible. Still, no need to give him a chance to hear her exhale, or to smell the onion on her breath from lunch.

Finally, Xyn stopped scanning the room and made for her desk to start searching it. From near her bed, she carefully hugged the wall until she was able to slip out the door that was still open, and into the hallway.

There was no worry of Xynka getting his paws on a working prototype; Cass had the only one in the station, possibly in the whole sector that the station administered. Plans, however, resided on her workstation. She'd started a full white noise crash rewrite of the workstation's drives, but she knew that any master spy—and Xynka was, without a doubt, one of the two most masterful spies she knew (the other being herself)—could salvage data from a drive that hadn't fully wiped itself yet, given enough time to work. It was almost a sure thing that she'd just lost one of Earth's biggest secrets; all she could do was to make use of the time she'd bought and steal back a different secret that would make this all worth it.

Xynka's quarters and her own were right around the corner from each other, so Cass didn't bother disabling her stealth field. It could stay on indefinitely (theoretically), so the only thing she had to worry about was some pedestrian not seeing her and getting bowled over by, subjectively, nothing. She kept to the walls and hacked her way into Xynka's suite with ease, only switching off the belt-mounted device once the door was closed behind her.

While humans preferred to utilize workstations with large drives for data storage, jendeer preferred stations that were mere processing and display, with files kept on external chips. They'd carry commonly used chips around with them —when Zynka had entered her room, he'd been wearing a decorative neckpiece with a bunch of chips stashed into it. The chip-and-display school of thought was hell on physical space requirements (entire cavernous buildings were dedicated to data storage and their equivalent of the postal service was one of their biggest industries) but when it came time to find a specific chip, it provided its own layer of obscurity. Cass couldn't just copy Xynka's drive to her own personal storage and be done with it.

Still, it was organized. She spent time combing through the (literal) folders, before realizing that JSEU's biggest secrets probably wouldn't be on a well-filed chip in the most logical, easy-to-find place. If it was instead intentionally misfiled or mislabeled, she'd never find it. She considered that Xyn might have been carrying it around on his neckpiece, but found that line of thought both unlikely and unhelpful.

Think. While at the moment they were trying to steal secrets from each other, Cassidy and Xynka were nonetheless friends. They'd worked together on assignments before and generally enjoyed each others' company, if at that arm's-reach distance that people in their profession often kept to. She didn't like how dirty it made her feel, but she'd wrestle with the guilt later; for now, *where would he keep a chip with data about subspace jump monopoly?*

She took a deep breath and forced herself to stand back and scan the room methodically. Stacks of data chips—already ruled out. Kitchenette—no, too easy to lose or break something with how haphazardly he threw his dishes around. *So glad we're not roommates.*

She went to his living area and took stock of what was there, trying not to recall the times they'd conversed, spoken conversations over light drinks, trying to tease unimportant secrets out of each other while respecting the big ones. She considered the couch—if nothing else looked promising, she could check the cushions like she was looking for loose change. His model collection—so fastidious compared to the kitchen, it—*wait.*

No.

Cassidy went to the long all-glass cabinet that acted as a wall bisecting the living area, in which was held models of different ships. Plenty of jendeer vessels, of course; but a smattering of ships from other species, particularly individual famous vessels. Cass herself had gifted him a model of the *TIV Vostok*, the vessel that had scouted behind shiwiik lines, discovered a weakness in their supply lines, and led to humanity's victory in their first and only interstellar war.

Among the other vessels, centered in the whole display and new since the last time Cass had been here, was a model of a *Hjrep*-class Jump Ferry. Jump Ferries were the only vessels large enough to sustain subspace rifts long enough to transit. The JSEU kept careful guard over subspace tech so nobody else could build Jump Ferries, and thus were the only company capable of moving people and cargo around the greater galactic community—effectively making the jendeer species as a whole the economic leaders of civilization.

Cass took the Jump Ferry out of the cabinet and examined it. A large, rounded-off hexagon, twice as long as it was wide, with infrastructure for running the vessel—quarters, engines, bridge, all the necessaries—in the back, and fully open in the front. Cargo barges were attached to the outside like lampreys, and the gantries inside were covered in greebles suggesting countless smaller vessels ready for a ride across space.

She removed a barge tentatively, to check if it contained a chip within it. What she found instead was a small metal contact, not a functional part of the physical connector, not magnetic. Electrical.

She checked the other barges. All with connectors. She peered close at the inside, and found traces of wiring.

Either the entire Jump Ferry was an integrated data chip hiding the secrets of economic monopoly or it lit up. Whichever it was, she was out of time; her implant softly pinged that Xynka had left her quarters and would be here in a minute, and she wouldn't even have time to find its plug (if it had one, *stupid, it probably just lights up and makes that damn jump noise*) and browse its files.

Cass re-enabled her stealth field. It struggled with the model in her hand, but as she held it close to her torso it was able to cloak that too. She stepped out, closing and locking the door behind her, and slid away as fast as she dared towards the Terran consulate. She spared a glance behind her and saw Xynka round the corner; she refocused forward, dodged pedestrians who didn't know she was there, and tried to just put as much distance as she could between herself and the jendeer spy.

She could see in her mind's eye Xynka noticing the missing Jump Ferry, and the look on his face at knowing his friend had betrayed him, consoled only by the fact that he'd also betrayed his friend. If photons were interacting with Cass right then, she would have been able to see the same look by glancing in a mirror (with two fewer eyes and less fur, of course).

She made it to a thoroughfare busy enough that remaining invisible would become a liability and ducked into a comm booth. There, she disabled her stealth field and rigged the belt up around the Jump Ferry model. When she re-enabled it, it cloaked the ship without issue, and if she held it far enough away from her it wouldn't try to cloak her as well. She exited the booth, trying to walk as normally as possible while holding something invisible away from one's body, which is to say she didn't quite succeed but most citizens didn't know human body language well enough, and frankly weren't paying enough attention, to know that anything was off. Certainly, Cassidy was the only one who bothered to notice her own hand flickering in and out of existence, and she sorely wished she hadn't.

The rest of the flight from the station was a blur. Once at the consulate, her credentials got her on the next Earth-bound ship with no fuss. It just missed the interval on a Jump Ferry headed to the human homeworld, and had to wait two more intervals to take a Ferry to Trappist, where a Ferry on the next interval would head to Earth. The massive, galaxy-wide Jendeeri Universal Interval System meant every single subspace jump happened at exact synchronized times, roughly six hours apart from each other, and ignored the solar clocks of almost every colony in the galaxy aside from their homeworld of Jendaaren; but it did make computing travel times with connecting flights a breeze. And besides, Xynka probably expected her to be on the direct-to-Earth flight, not taking a detour, which likely helped explain why no alarm was raised while she waited nervously.

Finally, nineteen hours after betraying her friend, she looked forward out of her ship, past the hundreds of other ships attached to gantries in front of it, through the open front hexagon of the full scale *Hjrep*-class Jump Ferry she'd ridden, and saw the blue marble of humanity's cradle.

* * *

A year later, humanity was attacked.

In the intervening time, Terran military and intelligence agencies had crunched the data that was, in fact, in the Jump Ship model. The tech turned out to be easy to replicate, but of course humanity needed to put their own spin on it. Exotic alloys were switched out for materials more common on Earth, making them cheaper to produce, and emissions created a different profile than JSEU drives but nothing was thought of it. Headway was being made on making it work on smaller ships too. First the big dreadnoughts, then large battleships, then mid-weight cruisers.

At first, jumps were always done during intervals; a human ship appearing in civilized space at the wrong time would arouse suspicion. But when going to, say, a secret shipyard and science facility being constructed in deep space —well, ships could come and go all day long. And the question wasn't *if* anyone would find out; it was *when* it'd be revealed, that humanity could operate Jump Ferries and more importantly license out smaller drives to whoever was willing to cough up the currency.

Cassidy was at Alpha Point, helping set up offices. She had been admonished for her presumed loss of stealth field technology, but her acquisition of subspace jump tech more than made up for it. Still, her promotion to office work seemed like quite the opposite to Cass, and she longed for field work again.

The attack came out of nowhere. The *TSV Marianas* arrived in-system, checked in, then immediately blew up. Then beams of energy lanced out and split another vessel, this one a military patrol boat, clear in half. Before they knew it, the defenders of the half-completed installations at Alpha Point were in a fight for their lives, a losing fight, against spindly black and red ships that tore them to shreds.

Maybe it was a fleet of the Jendeeri Police Fleet, arrived to punish humanity for stealing their tech. Maybe someone else found out and was jealous; but then how would they have gotten here without a Jump Ferry of their own? But the forms were unfamiliar and the capabilities beyond known science. Maybe it was a new species. Whatever it was, Earth needed to know, and a pack of ships made a break for the jump point. The battleship was destroyed, sliced up like a hot stick of butter. Cruisers fell, frigates popped, and science ships melted away. In the end, a single cruiser led a ragged flotilla creating a cluster of subspace rifts away from Alpha Point back to Earth.

But the unknowns followed.

Cassidy could only watch as the combined might of the Terran military and any other armed vessels humanity had in the system fought for their survival. They held the unknowns to a standstill, and then, inexorably, began to lose ground.

Non-human ships fled the system, gathering at the jump point. The one Jump Ferry in the system attempted to accommodate them all, stuffing itself to the gills. The next interval was hours away; navigation lockouts meant it was physically unable to jump until then, but it gave it time to take in as many ships as possible. As crews worked furiously, a subspace rift opened nearby. Crews of every species held their breath in terror, waiting for more unknowns to pour through and take out their rallying point, to ensure nobody would leave the system... but the rift closed again, with nothing emerging.

The human fighters were getting pushed back, their flotsam adding to the orbital detritus that had accompanied humanity's ascent to the stars. Ursa Station, one of the many terminus stations at the end of the space elevators needed to economically escape Earth's gravity well, was shredded, and the tether started to slowly whip to the side, fortelling unimaginable damage on the ground.

Caught between an ever-advancing rock and the hard place they called home, beleaguered defenders noticed new contacts behind the unknown fleet. They despaired; surely this was reinforcements in a final push to break their spirit.

The new contacts opened fire.

And caught unawares, a dreadnought in the unknown fleet erupted into a fireball.

Having dropped their stealth fields, the Jendeeri Police Fleet forces opened fire, and turned the tide of the battle.

* * *

Cassidy shuffled through reports of the talks that had taken place after the engagement. It wasn't necessarily in her job description, but she had enough pull to be kept in the loop, and she wanted to see what had resulted from her actions—and those of Xynka, when he had taken the stealth field tech that ended up coming to humanity's rescue.

A hold had been placed on all human subspace jumps; not under threat of force (though the human fleet was weakened and would have a hard time fighting back, for a time), but under the revelation that among the new emissions that humanity's re-engineering had created was mu-radiation, which acted as a sort of beacon for what the jendeeri referred to as "the Destroyers". Drawn by concentrations of mu-radiation, the Destroyers acted as some sort of cosmic, unknown force that inhibited interstellar travel. Only by using the rare alloys prescribed in the original blueprints could the emissions be kept to a low background level, and by using the intervals, mu-radiation emissions were kept to galaxy-wide distributed bursts, rather than concentrations as had happened at Alpha Point and Earth.

Armed with the ability to detect mu-radiation, human scientists leapt at the problem of eliminating mu-radiation entirely. Meanwhile the human innovation of smaller packaging was revolutionary—not to be released out to the public until the mu-radiation problem had been solved, but with that genie out of the bottle, the combined civilizations of the galaxy clamored for an end to JSEU's stranglehold on interstellar travel. Terran interests were the first to come out with their own Jump Ferries, utilizing original-spec subspace drives and operating on the interval, but it wasn't long until other politico-economic blocs christened their own.

Of course, just as the human re-engineering of jendeer technology came with drawbacks, it seemed only fair that the reverse would also be true.

* * *

What a surprise to meet you here?, Cassidy signed, indicating sarcastic punctuation at the end.

"Here" was in the middle of a hallway, traffic bustling past. At a point that, *coincidentally,* was equidistant from her own quarters and that of her counterpart.

Imagine that?, Xynka signed back, having picked up Cass' penchant for verbal irony. Though "verbal" wasn't quite the right word, anymore.

A different station, a few years later, and not quite

around the corner from each other anymore. But in between desk stints at the consulate, Cass occasionally got to engage in some rare instances of field work. It made her all nostalgic at times.

Especially when she got a top-secret tip that more jendeer technology was available to steal.

And especially when Xynka seemed to have gotten a similar message.

Personal scale shielding? Cassidy asked.

Xynka nodded. *Energy weapon breakthrough?*

Cass nodded back casually and held up a chip. *What say we work together this time.*

I'd appreciate not committing shiploads of naval officers to deafness from poorly adapted tech again, Xynka agreed, flashing a chip of his own from his neckpiece.

And maybe we can avoid summoning a cosmic horror again.

What, worse than humanity? Cass mock-gasped and lightly punched Xynka in the shoulder. The two friends joined hands, and set off to commit mutual treason, for the betterment of both their species.

Mutual Treason

Xynka had just finished licking his plate clean and was tossing it in the sink to sanitize later when his mail alert chimed. He crossed his kitchen to where a stubby partial wall separated it from the living room and pressed the heel of his paw against a lever, and a data chip dropped into his pads. It was unlabeled; the sort of thing that messages were sent on, received, wiped, then sent back out on all throughout jendeeri space. The lack of a sender tag was concerning, however.

He crossed to his workstation and plugged it in. Detecting the presence of the chip, the computer booted and ran the simple message algorithm on the chip, displaying it for Xynka. Or, rather, an absolute mess of Unicode characters which could be from any of some ten thousand languages from seventeen different species.

Physical chips being passed around gave the illusion of security, but Xyn knew that Pelottershek Station had received a transmission with a destination tag, dumped the transmission to a chip, and routed the chip to his quarters. Anyone could have intercepted the transmission, either in transit or even before it was sent to Pelottershek, and that's why encryption like this was used—the kind of encryption that Xyn could decode himself, but that scant few others could.

He pulled another data chip off his neckpiece and plugged it in. It ran a low-level decryption, the kind of thing that civilians wouldn't have access to but wasn't the hardest thing to decrypt, essentially whittling down the entirety of Unicode (a human standard, one of their many contributions to the bureaucratic efficiency of the galaxy) to the character set of a single language, in jendeeri script. A messy jumble, but almost familiar looking. Decently expected; many Jendeeri Information Bureau encryption schemes set that as the first step, and the resulting jumble was one that Xyn could now decrypt on his own.

It took him some time to do so. Character substitution—a couple of different methods to try, but eventually, done. This resulted in an obscure language that isolated communities of jendeer still spoke, one that Xyn was fluent in. But... it wasn't quite right. The words were familiar, but they didn't make sense in that context. He translated the text into Collective Jendeer to try a few more decryption schemata. In one—literally taking a chip of the latest edition of the P'hendreth University Collective Jendeer Dictionary and shifting every word down twelve entries—some sentences almost made sense. The fragments he got, and the difficulty of decryption, had at this point made him very nervous, his hearts pounding an alternating staccato in his chest. On a hunch, he went back to the original character decryption, and—after digging the appropriate chip up from its file folder—shifted *those* words down their respective dictionary (not updated nearly as recently; dying languages don't get the luxury of regular dictionary updates). That resulted in... well. More for double checking his work and allowing him a moment to take it in than any actual need to read it clearly, he translated into Collective, then sat back from his desk, looking at the workstation screen.

Read :: Destroy :: Proceed :: Acknowledge

Human technology (stealth field / personal) / present (Pelottershek Station [custody ^ Cassidy Scott])

Digital blueprint / confirmed

Physical prototype / suspected

Obtain (all) :: Immediate return (all) (personally)

Without even acknowledging that he'd received the message, he was to go and steal data and possibly hardware for something he hadn't even heard about until reading this. And he had to steal it... from Cassidy, his friend and/or rival, similarly employed as himself but for the Terran Intelligence Agency.

Well. Nothing to do but to get to it. He'd allowed himself a second to sit back and absorb; now it was past time to get to work. He pulled the chips out of his workstation and it powered back down. He then tossed the dictionary chip in a bowl for later re-filing and reattached the decryption chip to his neckpiece. Finally, he plugged the message chip into a surge port which fried the internals (and singed his fur while it was at it; nothing to do about it, time was of the essence), then pierced it with a canine tooth, then pocketed it; there was more he could do, but it would have to wait until after he'd stolen this mysterious human technology.

He left his quarters and worked his way quickly down

the hall and around the corner. Under the guise of keeping an eye on foreign intelligence agents, Xynka had ensured that Cass' cabin was close to his own suite. Usually though it was because they genuinely enjoyed each others' company. Keep your friends close, he remembered Cass saying about the arrangement, *and your enemies closer.*

He got to Cassidy's door and hit the panel for it to open; to his mild surprise, it opened on command, unlocked. Was she here? That'd make things difficult.

But no. He stood in the doorway, scanning the cabin. The workstation was on, but Cass was nowhere to be seen. Maybe the door had been locked after all and the station just recognized his access override immediately for once. Sure, that was it. Wait, had he locked his own door on the way out? He thought so but he wasn't positive. Even if he had, it'd stop almost anyone on the station *but* Cass. And she had no reason to get in there right now, right? She wasn't here. *She's not here.* She wouldn't know he wasn't in his quarters. *She's not here.*

After scanning the room for a minute too long, he stepped into the room and over to the workstation, the door behind him staying open a moment longer then sliding shut behind him.

He knew that humans preferred integrated onboard-storage computer systems rather than the chip-and-display system used by the jendeer (and just over half of the other species in the known galaxy). He'd used such "operating system" style workstations before, but it took him some time to realize what he was looking at on Cass' screen. Sector counts running up... pass two of seven... it was wiping its hard drive! Cass had known he was coming after all! She must have—*no*, stop this and get the data first. Then he could worry about Cassidy Scott.

He sat at the workstation and flexed his digits, taking

stock, trying not to panic. On a jendeer workstation he could just pull the chip with the data, but conversely a data chip could be completely wiped in mere seconds. The bits of metal and plastic in his pocket could attest to that. In this case the human workstation was a blessing; it gave him some time to work, as fast as he could with the almost-familiar human keyboard. He started by attempting to seize up its processes, but it kept chugging along, writing ones to the sectors of the drive. He grabbed an override chip from his neckpiece and plugged it in; in theory, it should stop the processor in its tracks and reboot the machine from the software on the chip. No luck; Xyn realized that it was overwriting the entire drive, including the operating system, so whatever process was running wasn't at the software level —there was some hardware, somewhere, telling the processor what to do.

He checked the rest of the ports on the front and back of the station, but nothing was plugged in aside from the input devices. There was a power cord though! He chastised himself and pulled it; all he needed was the drive, he didn't need to perform the data recovery on this workstation himself *in situ*.

The workstation, now disconnected from the wall, kept going, nearing the end of its third pass, alternating ones and zeros to the drive.

Battery.

Damn.

He removed the side cover from the machine. He could try to just pull the hard drive out; just because humans didn't use chip-and-display systems didn't mean that the data wasn't, after a fashion, removable. But a potential power surge (and burnt fur) could wipe the drive more surely than any methodical data wipe could. Xyn was left to wonder why that wasn't Cass' first option, and decided that, possibly, a fried drive might have some random data still intact.

Maybe it'd fry at the end of its seventh pass.

He looked up at the display. Starting its fourth pass, increasing numbers of ones and zeroes next to each other until repeating, probably a prime sequence. Someone had fun designing the wipe algorithm. Xyn wasn't having fun stopping it.

He looked at the motherboard for any anomalous chips that might be driving the data wipe. Nothing. He looked for something attached to the drive, maybe bypassing the workstation's hardware. Nothing. He looked again at the outside ports. Still nothing, just the input devices.

Wait.

He unplugged the keyboard.

The screen froze, then shut off.

He picked up the keyboard and looked it over. *What's a more convenient panic switch than a button that's already at your fingertips?* He carefully removed the drive and hoped he'd recovered it soon enough that jendeer xenotech data recovery specialists would be able to get what was needed. On a whim, he took the keyboard too; though he doubted it was anything overly complicated, it wasn't a countermeasure he'd run into before and it was surely worth something to somebody.

He left Cass' cabin and headed back for his own suite. Now that he'd recovered the drive—and hopefully the data thereon—he could spare a thought for the human agent. He hadn't considered, not for a moment, the prospect of not fulfilling the task set forth for him by his superiors. Now he took a moment to determine if he regretted his actions, and, no, he didn't. They both knew this was a possibility, and just as with other acquaintances he'd made along the way, he'd kept her at arm's length. He'd miss the friendly aspect to their rivalry, but he'd move on.

Maybe not immediately, but soon.

Xynka palmed the panel for his suite and the door unlocked and slid open. Again he scanned for Cass—she wasn't at his workstation, she wasn't rifling through his data chips, and besides, the most valuable chip in the suite, in the entire station, wasn't even—

Oh, FRELL.

* * *

Read :: Destroy
Human technology (stealth field / personal) / recovered

Human data storage (wiped) ^ digital blueprint

Data recovery / required

Physical prototype / not present

Cassidy Scott / not present

Cleaning :: en route

-Complication-

Data chip ^ digital blueprint (subspace drive) / missing

@ ^ Cassidy Scott / suspected

(this agent) Recall :: deliver human data storage :: offer resignation :: surrender for arrest

This was the message that preceded Xynka as he swept his suite of any remaining valuable intelligence and either disposed of it or clipped it to his neckpiece. Assuming he'd be afforded the privilege, he'd have to recover his model collection some other time, or start building it anew.

He assumed that, considering the true significance of his most recent acquisition and its subsequent loss, he would not in fact be afforded the privilege.

He sent another message to the station's spaceport to be on the lookout for a human matching Cass' description trying to make the next Jump Ferry to Earth but didn't hold out much hope. Depending on the efficacy of whatever this stealth field technology was, she could bypass any security checkpoint and have her pick of ships with nobody, not even the crew, any the wiser.

And finally, he boarded a personal flitter—hardly more than a starfighter with a passenger seat—piloted by a Bureau agent and set home for Jendaaren, to deliver the data, his report, his resignation and, should he choose to even offer one, his defense.

Surprisingly, however, his superiors only accepted the first two. Oh, to be sure there was a lot of noise made, how could he lose such valuable intel, what form was it even in, wait why did he have it in the first place, who made *that* decision, and outrage and uncertainty rang up and down the halls of the Bureau, ultimately fizzling out without anyone losing so much as a paycheck over it.

It was about the time that he was tasked with the operational security of the labs working on stealth tech—because, yes, due to molecular alignment, or something undoubtedly quantum, the data had been, to some extent, recovered, and needed only some relatively simple legwork to get the gaps plugged up, then the real fun, it was said, could begin—that Xyn considered the possibility that someone had *intentionally* leaked subspace travel technology to a foreign power, quite possibly to humans specifically via the relationship that he had formed with one of their best agents. Xyn had been *set up* to lose this tech, so the reasoning went, and if that were the case then he was grateful that whoever this traitor was, they had at least exerted the common courtesy to keep Xyn's tail out of the coals.

Xynka's work at the lab complex was a far cry from what he'd been doing previously, but good security consultants became so by knowing all the ways that a system could be attacked, and could therefore anticipate incursions from multiple conceptual angles; and Xynka's previous work had made him a very good security consultant. After the labs were set up, it was almost a quiet posting.

Almost. It was quiet indeed from a security standpoint; he stayed vigilant, rotated out those under him who got hopelessly complacent, and had nary a search network bot come sniffing at his firewalls.

But then, it wasn't a quiet posting, because stealth field technology was just so damn *loud*.

The labs had started by recreating the blueprints as best they could reproduce them. That meant a belt that one would wear with machinery woven into it, and a somewhat chunky box to one side of the clasp. At this person-sized scale, the belt let out a quiet yet still audible hum. Not much use, that, since most species would be able to hear it. But then, sound doesn't transmit in a vacuum, so what about scaling it up a bit?

It was clear from the blueprints that humans hadn't scaled the technology at all, so this was new ground. New and noisy; the volume of the sound generated ramped up commensurately with the volume the field was meant to contain. Hiding a flitter in a docking bay made it hard for anyone nearby to hold a conversation; making photons dance around a corvette was uncomfortable verging on painful; and crews of larger vessels had permanent hearing damage to look forward to if they were stealthed for long.

Curiously, the labs were told to install what they had onto a small fleet, testing long enough to confirm it'd work, then keeping the prototypes installed rather than continually experimenting on them. "Iterate," they were told, "but who knows when we'll have need of them."

Someone did know, apparently. Because shortly after the fleet was outfitted, it was mobilized.

Xynka, the ranking Bureau member on-site, received the dossier. And couldn't believe the in-flight briefing he was about to give.

* * *

"Why the rush?" Xynka heard as he entered the briefing room. "The next interval isn't for another two hours."

"In two hours it will be too late." Xyn responded as he took his position on a dais at the front of the room. He locked eyes with the officers present, of the *Hidden Tooth*—flagship of this small fleet—and the remote holographic avatars of officers on the other ships, all of which were rigging onto the gantries of a (relatively) small Jump Ferry.

"That is why the *Dawnbringer's* navigation system is not synced to the interval," he continued once he had everybody's attention. "As soon as everyone is attached, we're jumping."

Gasps went up in the room. A jump off the interval? Madness!

"We're pressed for time so excuse me if I keep things simple. Does anyone know why we adopted the interval in the first place?"

"To ease travel schedules."

"Side effect."

"To balance... some sort of emissions?"

"Yes, Lieutenant, correct. Mu-radiation. Why is it important that this be evenly distributed?" He saw someone almost put a paw up, who then thought better of it. Xyn locked eyes with the officer and said, "No stupid answers."

The officer swallowed, then hesitantly said, "The Destroyers?"

Laughs went up in the room. The officer who said it looked embarrassed, until she saw that Xyn wasn't laughing; then her fur seemed to grow three shades paler.

"Yes. The Destroyers. Thought by our ancestors to punish us for taking to the stars. Thought to be the retribution for space-bound hubris. We found out long ago that they're attracted by mu-radiation. So we spread it out, so there isn't a target. So we keep our Jump Ferries large and move as much mass as possible for every jump. And we were so successful that the Destroyers faded to myth and children's fables, and because we used the interval, and kept that technology to ourselves, they stayed there.

"Then..." Xyn sighed, a note more theatrically than was strictly needed. "Then, humans happened."

A nervous chuckle went around the room as he steadied his voice before continuing, "Somehow, humans have obtained subspace jump technology and have been testing it with... enthusiasm. We wouldn't have even known until some old mu-radiation buoys started showing off-interval readings." (This was absolute truth, and also a convenient excuse to "discover" humanity's use of the tech.) "The readings seemed like a bug at first, but no. And that's why we know where we're going—a deep-space facility of some sort. And none too soon." He pushed another image to everybody's displays. "An hour ago we got confirmation of transverse polarization of the mu-radiation pattern.

"The Destroyers are back. And it's up to us to pull the humans' tails out of the coals."

He nodded at the *Hidden Tooth's* captain, who took Xyn's place at the dais and said to the rest of the room, "Alright, you heard the spook! The primates got hold of fire and are gonna burn themselves, and we're gonna slap it out of their paws. To your stations. Is everyone linked up?"

Most of the remote holos nodded; the last one held up a digit, fuzzed slightly, then said, "Just finished."

"Great. *Dawnbringer* bridge? Let's get to this deep space lab."

"Agent?" called the comms officer. "Message for you." He handed Xyn a message chip.

Xynka frowned and plugged it into a nearby reader, scanning it quick. It'd better be important, to come in...

... "Captain? We're going to have to set a new course."

* * *

Xynka stood on the bridge, out of the way. He was no longer directly involved in the execution of the operation, having delivered his briefing, but his presence and firsthand account would still be valuable to the Bureau.

Xyn looked out of the bridge viewports, the *Hidden Tooth* dropping away in front, then the expanse of the *Dawnbringer*, which the *Tooth* was attached to the side of. The rest of the fleet was holed up inside the hollow vessel. In front of all of them, a bright subspace rift was opening.

"*Dawnbringer*, forward. All ships, stealth on my mark." The captain watched as the rift drew closer, then just as the prow of the Jump Ferry brushed up against the rift, he said, "Crews, brace; MARK!"

Normally, a subspace transit sounds like the ship is getting stressed slightly. Some creaking, a twisting sensation felt as much as heard for a couple seconds until emerging on the other side of the portal.

This time, it sounded like... it sounded awful. There was no sound like it, nothing grounded in Xynka's experience. It was pain, like none he'd ever known, even through the hearing protection everybody was wearing.

The fleet emerged and a yellow icon with a black slash across it appeared on the screen of every crew member in the fleet. *Detach :: proceed*, in the hastily agreed-upon visual parlance they'd set out ahead of time. As they did, the bridge crews looked out and saw not some deep space outpost, but the blue orb of Earth in front of them. Nearby, a civilian Jump Ferry was facilitating an evacuation from humanity's homeworld. And ahead... the stuff of nightmares. Of children's stories. The stuff that may have destroyed countless civilizations until the jendeer learned, not how to defeat them, but how to hide from them.

The Destroyers, attacking the defense fleet of humanity.

Magenta indicators lit up on the Captain's screen; when enough ships indicated they were free of the *Dawnbringer*, he sent the next command. Red and white; *flank*.

And when everybody sent another magenta confirmation, a flag of teal and tan, then teal and red. *Reveal :: attack*.

The pain stopped as the *Hidden Tooth* turned off its stealth field, and while the ambush was messy—some crew likely fully incapacitated by this point—it was still effective, catching the destroyers unawares. The humans surged forward in return, and the battle unfolded in a silent ballet.

Wait, aren't there supposed to be auditory simulators? Why don't I hear anything? Why aren't the crew communicating?

Oh. He looked around and saw that many crew members were bleeding from their ears, indeed trying to shout to each other, but neither Xyn nor the rest of the bridge crew could hear. They sometimes were able to flag someone else's attention, and attempt a sort of somatic communication. And somehow, they prevailed, and soon the final ship in this vanguard of the Destroyers broke up, its pieces spinning away from each other.

They had prevailed.

* * *

A few years later, Xynka—decorated for his part in obtaining stealth technology for the jendeer and in bringing the rescue fleet to the defense of humanity—was enjoying a sort of retirement on Femrehsser Station, a desk posting as more of a formality to fill his time than for processing any crucial work. It wasn't that the deaf had no place in the Jendeeri Information Bureau, just that Xynka had expressed his desire to retire and he was too valuable to fully let go of.

Cassidy was also on the station, likewise none the worse for wear for Xyn having taken the technology she'd been custody to. Xyn was very happy that they had been able to catch back up and reforge their friendship. They were even able to talk a bit more openly, their respective secrets revealed to (stolen by) each other and, if in fact if not in methodology, known to the greater galaxy.

And so it was that, after licking his plate clean and tossing it into the sink, a panel lit up, presumably accompanied by a noise of some sort but Xyn didn't know and long ago stopped caring. He pressed the heel of his paw against a lever, and a data chip dropped into his pads. It was unlabeled.

The decryption was familiar; he'd used it only once before in his life.

Read :: Destroy :: Proceed :: Acknowledge

Human technology (energy defense shield / personal) / present (Femrehsser Station [custody ^ Cassidy Scott])

Digital blueprint / confirmed

Physical prototype / suspected

Obtain (all) :: Immediate return (all) (personally)

He leaned back and looked at the message. Identical wording, identical encryption. Identical instructions to do the thing first and ask questions later.

And he'd just received blueprints for another proprietary piece of jendeeri technology.

He considered responding to the message, but shook his head. He fished the blueprint chip from a potted plant, clipped it to his neckpiece, and left his quarters. He had a meeting to attend.

Mutual Treason Glossary: Jendeeri Punctuation Guide

:: - "and then", dictating a sequence of events to happen.

(attribute) - More complex adjectives and attributes of the subject under discussion, but not the most important. Can nest. While subjects of sentences are usually gleaned by context, this can specify a subject at the beginning of a statement, particularly a string of verbs.

/ - "has attribute", clarifying the state of something beyond simple adjectives - typically reserved for the most pertinent attribute.

^ - "is in possession of", can refer to a person or an inanimate object ("water ^ glass", for instance).

@ - Shorthand to refer to the same subject as the previous statement.

-Word- - A new topic not related to the previous discussion. Think of it as a heading for a paragraph break.

ACKNOWLEDGEMENTS

I of course need to thank my various advance readers, catching mistakes here and there, but special consideration goes to Adam Bertocci, the first person to behold this mess. I distinctly remember being at work shooting video and my phone buzzing nonstop, and glancing at the notifications to see "Adam has made 206 suggestions" in the first hour and a half. He didn't stop there and the book is better for his feedback (as well as more conformant to proper writing and punctuation; anything you notice is due to my own stubbornness). He is the author of *Two Gentlemen of Lebowski: A Most Excellent Comedie and Tragical Romance* as well as many short stories that can be found on Kindle. He is also an accomplished filmmaker and screenwriter. Check him out, tell him I sent you.

Also big thanks to Alison Bugenis, who gave me the motivation to power through the last few chapters when I wasn't quite sure how they'd get where they needed to go. Writing sprints are a dangerous tool, Allie. Use them wisely.

ABOUT THE AUTHOR

Andrew Bugenis is a YouTube creator, Twitch streamer, filmmaker, voice actor, and former bookseller. He grew up on *Star Wars* and enjoys creating new worlds to play in. His short film, Breakdown at 238 Hypatia, has been nominated for awards at numerous film festivals. He can be found online at most websites under the user name BoterBug.

Made in the USA
Middletown, DE
04 November 2022

14043137R00149